I0766990

Dedicated to the creative spirit
& enduring friendship

Praise for "Baltimore Sideshow"

Cottle and Rowan form a dynamic duo of word and image, illustrating and illuminating the lost treasures of Baltimore's unique and often freakish history. Both words and images range from coarse to subtle, tender to gross. We have success here in this collaboration as words without images and images without words would fail to present this complete picture of "Charm City's" refined yet macabre past. Flip through this survey of strangeness and let your finger fall where it may. This well researched and cleverly crafted compilation entertains, fascinates and will not fail to delight sober professors or Natty Bo inebriated undergrads alike. "Baltimore Sideshow" is a "charming" look at "Bawlmer's" flawed superheroes and their incubator, this strange and utterly unique city called "Baltimore."

—Ryan Tkac, Artist and Musician, Maryland Institute College of Art, '01

Katherine Cottle captivates by using poetry to peel back the layers and tell the tragic tale of Axl Rotten. She proves that while his choices may have been ugly, his heart was anything but.

—Brian Soscia, Former Wrestler, Radio Show Creator and Host @ THEBrianSoscia of The Soscia Network Radio Show/Philadelphia/Wilmington

"Baltimore Sideshow" prompts readers to become aquainted with some of this city's quirky and disturbing personalities. Rather than depicting these people as sideshows, Cottle presents them as creators. Her exquisitely rendered formal poems—each form chosen for a specific personality—give these characters voices. The art work by Shannon Rowan accompanying each poem illustrates their accomplishments and their dreams. Ultimately, Baltimore Sideshow takes us on a journey through 20th century Baltimore and the people who subtly, sometimes silently, shaped the city.

—Michelle Tokarczyk, Author of *Working-Class Women in the Academy* and *Bronx Migrations*

"Baltimore Sideshow" is a stunningly original and deeply affecting collaboration. Each paired poem and illustration are vivid shards pulled from the kaleidoscope of humanity, exploring with empathy and compassion the rich complexity of each individual life, while at the same time illuminating the elemental aspects of our shared experience. Cottle's exquisite poetry and Rowan's rich illustrations complement one another beautifully, with words and images echoing back and forth, adding layers of resonance to the incredible stories of five historical figures. A treasure to be read and re-read, with new gems of vision and understanding waiting to be uncovered on each journey.

—Sara Kelleher, LCSW-C, graphic designer and novelist

Paperback edition first published in the USA in 2020 by
Shannon Rowan & Katherine Cottle

Hardback edition first published in the USA in 2020 by
Shannon Rowan & Katherine Cottle

Written by Katherine Cottle

Illustrated by Shannon Rowan

ISBN: 978-1-913438-31-9

Baltimore
SIDESHOW

While 21st century "sideshows" are now readily available on our mobile phones and computerized devices, it was only a couple of decades ago that "sideshows" were still primarily found in public settings. If the following historical figures were born today, they would certainly not be the "sideshows" they were considered to be in their day, due to progressions of public opinion and policy regarding disability, sex, gender, violence, addiction, and race.

For good and for bad, for profit and for exploitation, for pleasure and for pain, willingly and unwillingly, the following "sideshows" became a part of the century that began with the mass distribution of the automobile for human connection and ended with the mass connection of the Internet for human distribution.

What many do not realize is that these memorable "sideshow" figures had their own "sideshows": creative venues which housed artistic passions and lives outside of the spotlight of barkers, owners, directors, managers, and doctors. From direct self-display to unacknowledged spectacle, the following Baltimore "sideshows" now tell their own "sideshow" stories—for a 21st century audience to see and to hear.

Come *Inside* . . .

Here you will find the sideshows of:

*the Most Remarkable Man Alive,
the Belle of the Block,
the Drag Queen of the Century,
a Global Wrestling Champion,* and
the first human immortal cell line.

Johnny Eck

Johnny Eck, born John Eckhardt, Jr. on August 27, 1911 in East Baltimore/Highlandtown, arrived without any legs and only reached 18 inches tall during his lifetime. Eck's twin brother, Robert, was born full-bodied and lived with Eck as a companion for the duration of their lives. Johnny appeared in the 1932 cult classic, *Freaks*, and traveled with various circuses as a sideshow feature throughout much of his young adulthood, at which time he was billed "The Most Remarkable Man Alive."

After sideshows became passé in the mid-20th century, Eck worked in various capacities, including running an arcade and conducting the train on a children's ride in a local park in Baltimore. After a break-in in 1987, in which two thieves robbed and physically assaulted Eck and his brother, Eck became reclusive. Eck died in his sleep from a heart attack at age 83 on February 25, 1995 in his childhood home at 622 North Milton Avenue.

Eck was a gifted painter, model-maker, photographer, and visual artist, as well as a gymnast, swimmer, race car driver, magician, and stuntman. He learned the skill of screen painting from local grocer William Oktavec, who invented the form in Baltimore in 1913. The colorful screens allowed residents a shield from the hot summer sun, as well as increased privacy.

SCREENS

Poetic Form: Like the square canvas of Eck's screens, the Shakespearean sonnet utilizes a restricted space (1/2 a page), a strict rhyme pattern (ABAB/CDCD/EFEF/GG), and a prescribed number of lines (14). The sonnet also mimics Eck's physical body in its top-heavy construction of three four-line stanzas, followed by a two-line couplet—which must hold the weight of the poem through the amplification, refutation, or conclusion of the previous stanzas.

Artistic Medium: Linoleum cuts printed with black ink, based on Eck's screen prints. Chosen to create black and white abstract graphic representations of Eck's work which was simple in its approach and form, the process involves cutting into linoleum blocks (similar to wood cuts) and then inking the blocks before transferring to paper.

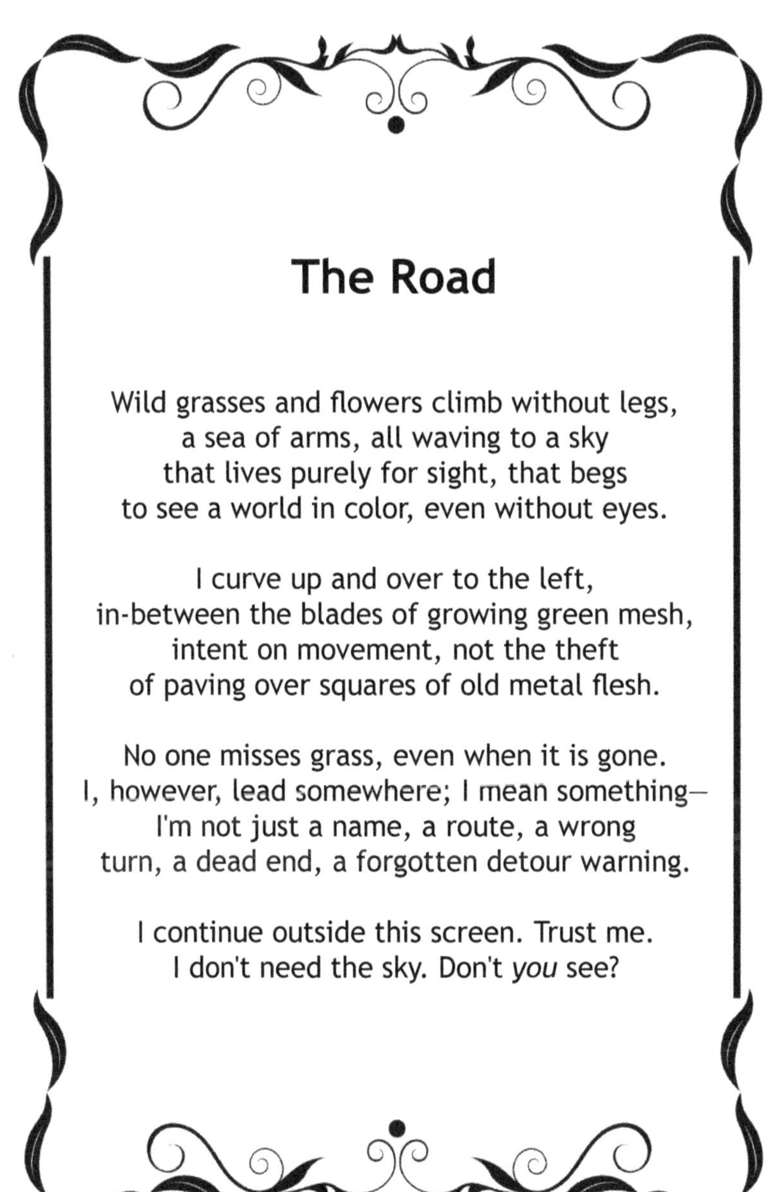

The Road

Wild grasses and flowers climb without legs,
a sea of arms, all waving to a sky
that lives purely for sight, that begs
to see a world in color, even without eyes.

I curve up and over to the left,
in-between the blades of growing green mesh,
intent on movement, not the theft
of paving over squares of old metal flesh.

No one misses grass, even when it is gone.
I, however, lead somewhere; I mean something—
I'm not just a name, a route, a wrong
turn, a dead end, a forgotten detour warning.

I continue outside this screen. Trust me.
I don't need the sky. Don't *you* see?

Jesus

It isn't hard to stay still in this position,
that is, unless I forget. Don't
worry, I will keep hold while you fashion
me the way you like, I won't

move, or talk, or sweat, or breathe.
I won't blink, or dream, or curse, or sin.
I'm okay for awhile. I promise I won't leave.
Take your time. Make my skin

slightly rough like yours, make my face
paused in thought like yours, make my brow
hold the weight of the places
only a few lucky ones get to know.

Make me end there—below my waist.
God's son. Just that. No waste.

Jesus Gives the FU

Just warning you, though, there might be some days
I want to keep all of the fish to myself,
some days that I need to get away.
Go ahead—take over the nets, the burdens, the wealth.

I'm just fine here on land;
walking on water is overrated, too many mosquitoes,
the glare always hurts my eyes. Really, the sand
is ten times softer on my feet and toes.

I'll get back to business one day.
For now, you can just pretend that I am waving.
From a distance it's all the same anyway.
I'm just a man in a robe, watching you, saving

you even if you don't want me to.
Sorry, dude, that's just what fishermen do.

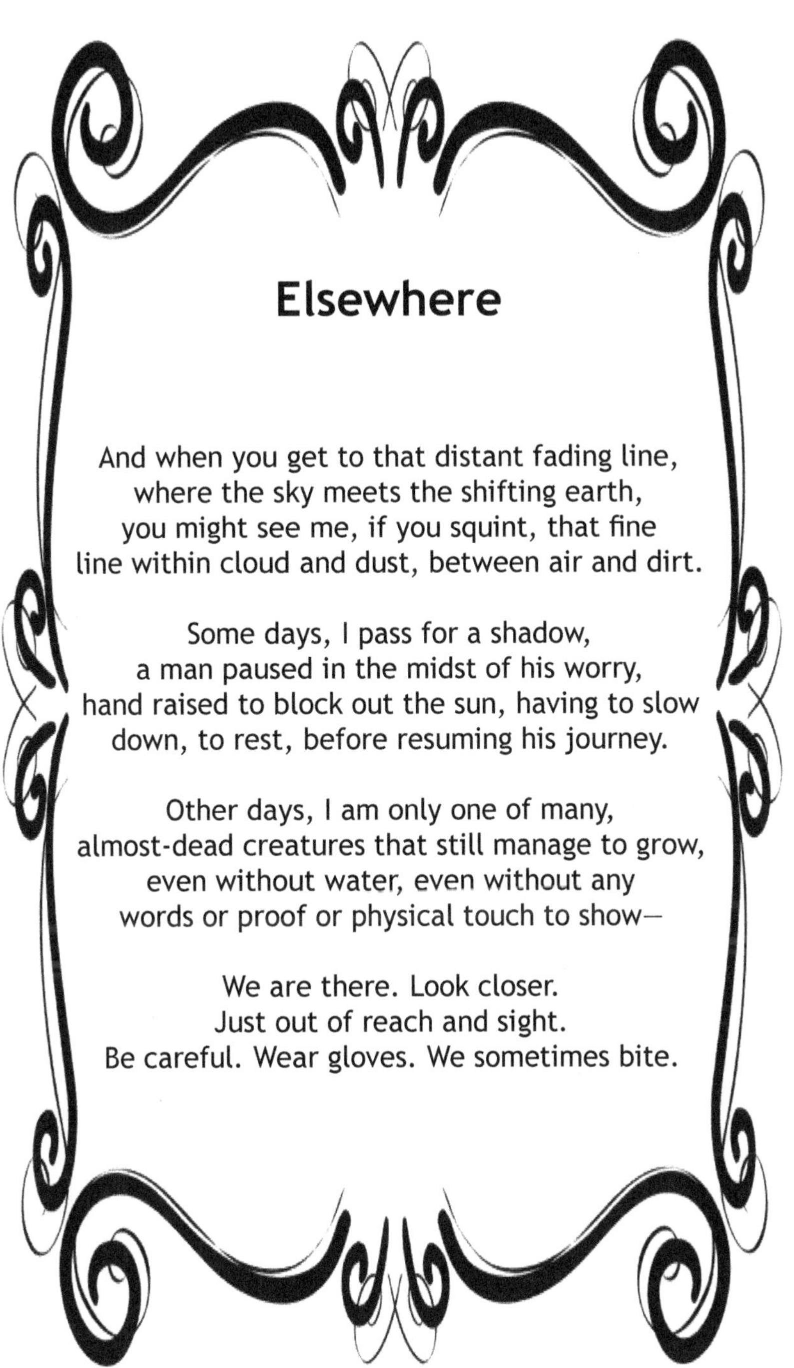

Elsewhere

And when you get to that distant fading line,
where the sky meets the shifting earth,
you might see me, if you squint, that fine
line within cloud and dust, between air and dirt.

Some days, I pass for a shadow,
a man paused in the midst of his worry,
hand raised to block out the sun, having to slow
down, to rest, before resuming his journey.

Other days, I am only one of many,
almost-dead creatures that still manage to grow,
even without water, even without any
words or proof or physical touch to show—

We are there. Look closer.
Just out of reach and sight.
Be careful. Wear gloves. We sometimes bite.

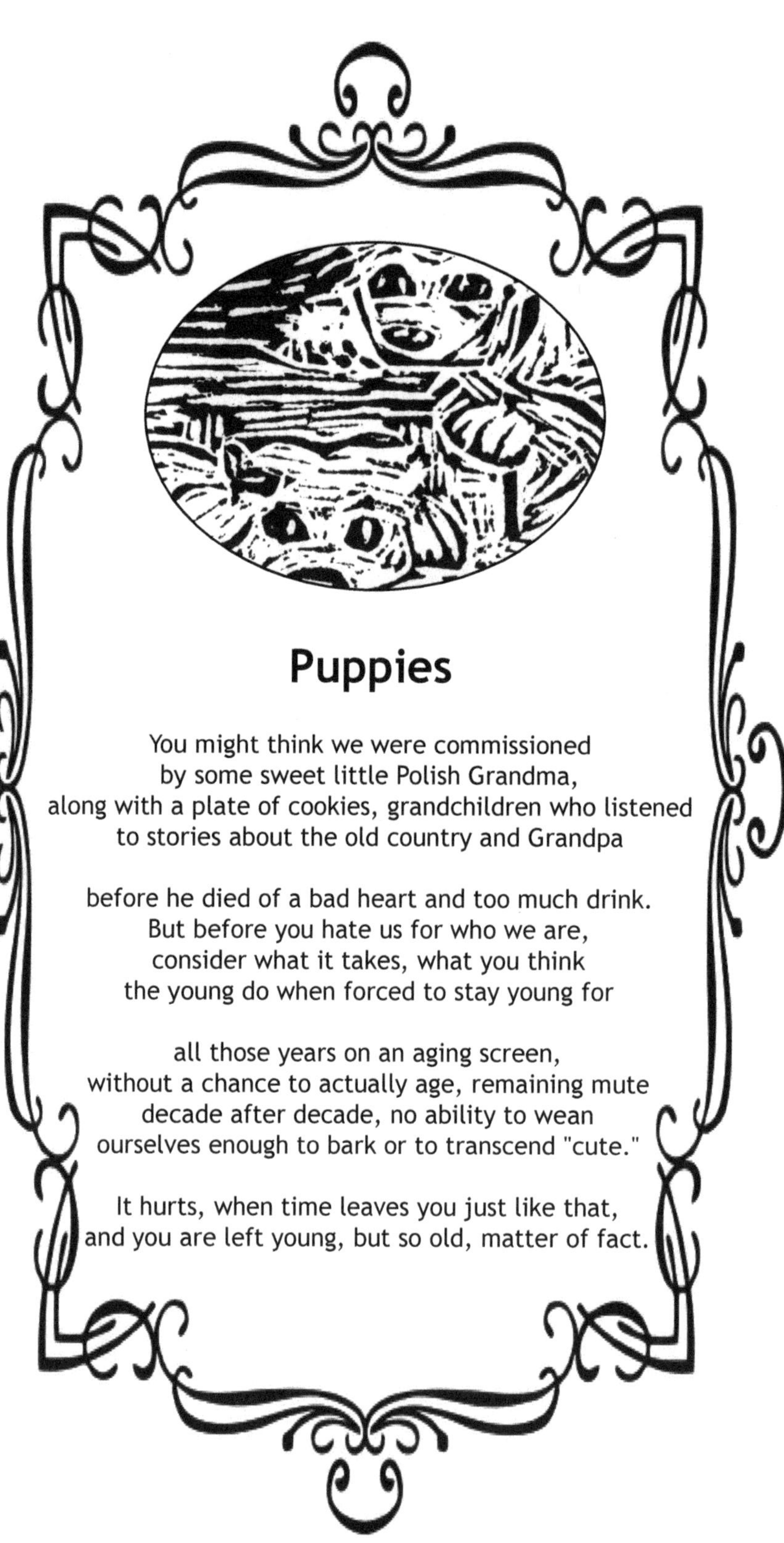

Puppies

You might think we were commissioned
by some sweet little Polish Grandma,
along with a plate of cookies, grandchildren who listened
to stories about the old country and Grandpa

before he died of a bad heart and too much drink.
But before you hate us for who we are,
consider what it takes, what you think
the young do when forced to stay young for

all those years on an aging screen,
without a chance to actually age, remaining mute
decade after decade, no ability to wean
ourselves enough to bark or to transcend "cute."

It hurts, when time leaves you just like that,
and you are left young, but so old, matter of fact.

Kittens

You'd be mistaken to think we were nervous,
balanced next to one another like two sides
of the same design, our dual purpose
somewhere in the background, somewhere besides

here, in a room, with nothing to do.
You can look all you want.
There's nothing to see—just two brothers who
found a way to stay in one line, who wanted

nothing more than to find a way
to live out both of our nine lives.
Not content with one, or twelve, we're staying
here, in this frame, where time survives.

We've made it past expectancy, just by sticking together.
We've made it this far, even with the damn weather.

Fell's Point

Funny, how things look so little in the distance,
how the light can shrink a house to a few
slivers of rope, tiny ribbons glistening
within the rocking port—unfurling red, green, blue.

Reach your hand out. Touch where we meet,
where the wet damp of my heart tugs through the blur
of the deep, way past the two hundred feet
that hide what isn't seen, what might have occurred.

If you listen closely enough you might still hear
the sounds: sputter of oil, suction of mud,
wind whistling past wood planks in the salted air.
It's a story that goes way back, that could

keep going, I imagine, for many years,
yet pauses today, tangled among these hopes and fears.

Scene

There is a house, on the other side of a fence,
where real people live, behind windows and doors
though they never come out, not even
to feed the ducks, pick flowers, or run toward

a sky that never rains, that never pours.
Rather, royal blue only fills in what is left
after the rest is finally painted, after the colors
have dried and settled, content except

for the shivers that never end. Kisses of cold
street air climb marble steps to reach through
windows, through doors which open and close
into long nights of more of the same; although,

if you close your eyes, you might find me there—
on the other side, too neat to be found anywhere.

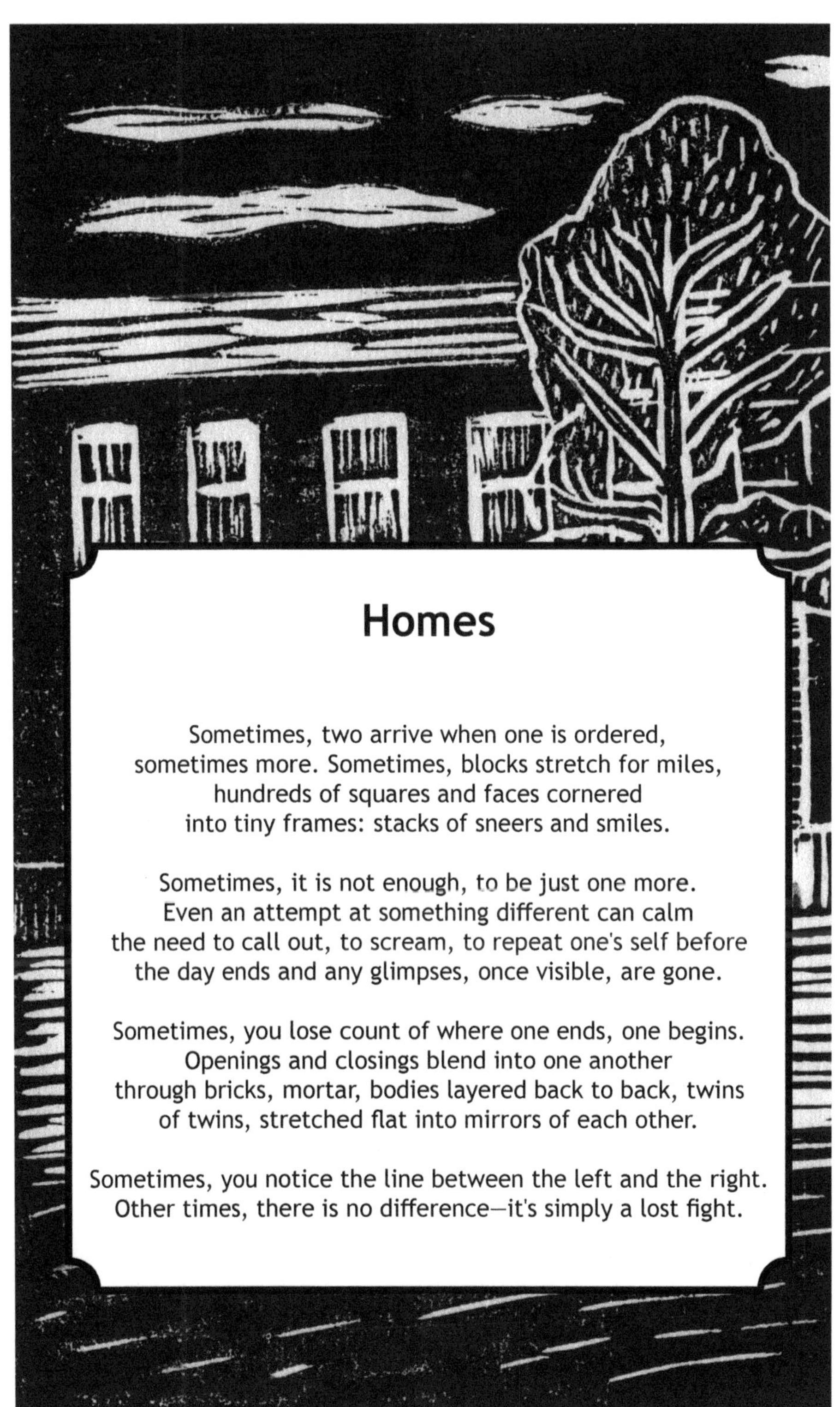

Homes

Sometimes, two arrive when one is ordered,
sometimes more. Sometimes, blocks stretch for miles,
hundreds of squares and faces cornered
into tiny frames: stacks of sneers and smiles.

Sometimes, it is not enough, to be just one more.
Even an attempt at something different can calm
the need to call out, to scream, to repeat one's self before
the day ends and any glimpses, once visible, are gone.

Sometimes, you lose count of where one ends, one begins.
Openings and closings blend into one another
through bricks, mortar, bodies layered back to back, twins
of twins, stretched flat into mirrors of each other.

Sometimes, you notice the line between the left and the right.
Other times, there is no difference—it's simply a lost fight.

Lucky (Eck's Last Screen Painting)

I could be a kitten, or a puppy, or maybe a man,
some creature small enough to squeeze in-between
the holes of a screen, to reach unreachable lands
not found on maps, located beyond what is seen.

Dressed for my time, I'll hold this pose if you like,
even if my arms ache from the weight, from being part
of a museum, of storage, a past oddity not unlike
the childhood I remember, a place now only found in art.

I've discovered the gold, yes, but it's starting to rot,
which is what happens when treasures aren't claimed,
when they sit, untouched, in their silver pots.
Look closer, you'll see the blood, I'm ashamed

to say isn't mine, but the last little man's, who's
forgotten, who, I must admit, is now simply old news.

Blaze Starr

Blaze Starr, born Fannie Belle Fleming on April 10, 1932 in Wayne County, West Virginia, first performed at the 2 O'Clock Club in Baltimore's infamous red light district section, "The Block," in 1950. Her "blazing" red hair and comedic burlesque performances were her trademarks, including the creative use of unexpected stage props, such as a baby black panther and a combustible couch. Starr caught the attention of Louisiana governor, Earl Long, with whom she would sustain a long-term affair until his death in 1960. Starr purchased the 2 O'Clock Club in 1968 and owned and operated it for over two decades.

In 1983, Starr officially retired from the burlesque business and devoted her time to creating hand-crafted jewelry. For a few years she sold her jewelry out of the Carrolltown Mall in Eldersburg, Maryland, and then exclusively sold her work online. Starr passed away at age 83 on June 15, 2015 near her hometown in West Virginia.

GEMS

Poetic Form: *The nesting rhyme seems the perfect form for a "burlesque" poem. Like the gradual reveal and undressing of a burlesque dancer, the nesting rhyme form unpeels its layers, or final word, as it progresses through each three-line stanza. In order to replicate the different acts of a traditional burlesque show, the number of stanzas also gradually depletes with each poem in this series—eventually leaving a single stanza with one stripped rhyme.*

Artistic Medium: *Black watercolor paint on paper. Watercolor was chosen to create soft lines, fluidity, and realism to reflect Starr's sensuality, as well as that of her jewelry featured on her website.*

**Clear Aurora Borealis on a
Gold-Plated Filigree Hanger**

It isn't how we delicately hang that mesmerizes,
rather how we move, how the projected light rises
and falls against us, teasing you. Who says

we are out of reach, unattainable,
only temporarily available for those tenable
in their want, or rich, or connected, or able

to reach the places beyond satisfaction
and the insatiable pull of inactive action,
where most reside, each day, barely holding on?

I won't tell you what I know: my understanding
that the light is set above us, the stage-hand standing
to the left knows the exact angle needed to lure you in.

I know you already know how it is to manipulate,
how it is part of the job, nothing more, a plate
passed down the hard wood pew, then guiltily ate

with stones that only impress on certain occasions.
Most of the time, we are put away, cased in
the daily duties of waiting for the next son-

of-a-bitch to tell us about his undying admiration
for what lies behind our dangling parts, to ration
his own life into parts, mainly—off and on.

But we wouldn't want it any other way, otherwise
we wouldn't shine with such brilliance, only wise
up, pack our bags, close our wide-opened eyes.

And that isn't possible for us; the gold-plated filigree
may not be real, but it does the job, most agree.
We know the cheap metal underneath is practically free;

we'll pretend anyway, let you imagine the Aurora Borealis
are here just for you, lights like no other, roaring real as
your fantasies, as clear as love really ever is.

Welcome! If you are into mammals, or amphibians, fetishes
of any sort, stick around. You might be interested in Turtle, she's
only 150 million years old, still young enough, that is

unless you are into chubbier ones, in which case I'd recommend
Elephant, who sings lovely and twirls her trunk on command.
Okay, not your thing, I've got others in my trunk; men

die for Fish, she's a smooth one, fast and slippery,
escapes right through your hands, her scales woven purely
with exotic silk. Bonus: She never sleeps, never needs to re-

charge. In fact, some say she's almost iridescent,
all shades blended together and dipped into one long distant
chain of colors; she's breath-taking, truly heaven-sent.

Perhaps you prefer the modern, the minimal; however,
there's nothing like natural hair to warm you at night, whether
it's Bear's full body bristling with an entire coat of fur or

the molded mane running down Horse's neck, fingering
the muscles that tighten as she gallops around the ring.
Unlike Bear, she passes those who cannot keep up, who stay in

stride alongside her until the last lap, when they surrender.
Count on her to reach the finish line. She'll never render
herself second or third—guaranteed! Today, though, to end or

to lose is irrelevant, for there's Frog, who pleases everyone.
A consistent croaker with a crazy-long tongue, the very one
known to be a royal in disguise. If nothing else, she's the one.

The hard part might be picking. You're speechless, proclaiming
all to be your preference? Well, I've included them all, claiming
nothing more than 2 ft. of beauties, all ready for your aiming.

**Amethyst and Hematite
with Six Mother of Pearl Fetishes 24"**

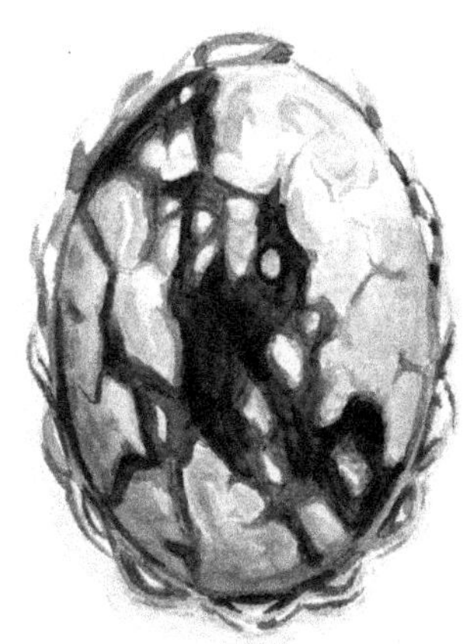

Snowflake Obsidean on Silver-Plated Clips

Notice my borders, the fluted silver-plated clips, encasing
black worlds, my white droplets floating through space, casing
for a place to root, to stick, before attempting to settle in.

Soon enough you'll forget anyway—what's keeping us together,
how there can't be an inside without an outside; you'll profess either
here or not here, forgetting the distance found between there.

I'm a universe that keeps expanding, one that tricks you into believing
I can be captured within two polished stones, dual orbits leaving
their trace of lost and undiscovered places. You may even

locate yourself among my planets, scattered without any pattern,
next to the small moon in the top corner, showing the wrong turn
you took before you found yourself here, alone, eager to earn

a passage into the arms of fire, earth, and water. I'm obsidian,
which means "bastard child" (my true birth), made inside an
angry relationship which had to dissolve, too flammable in

its raw form to ever survive. That's what happens, regardless,
when two forces collide and cannot let go of their guard, lest
they cannot crystallize; instead, something new cries (no less

beautiful than its former parts) sharp and shiny, amorphous
and translucent. But we won't take the credit, no more fuss
is necessary, just take us home: watch us, polish us, protect us.

When our smoke starts to rise, remember you, too, are combustible,
so slow down, take your time. Let the elements take over, table
your search for the stars. We're on top of it, literally—ready and able.

There is something to be said, for wearing the ocean
and the earth around your neck. Please don't shun
us because we're found in seaside stores; we're just an

easy marketed attempt to pay tribute to what came before.
Before seaside and tourist stores grew, we were used for
palace domes, for extravagant masks, for amulets, or

protection from evil. Decorative and ancient, turquoise
swims in its own mineral ponds, a blue-green koi
on display for all to see upon entry. The truth is,

we may not be precious, but we can still call attention
to ourselves, still dig up the past—the remaining tension
of a people erased, for others' own good, left for dead on

stones that continue to climb over hills and graveyards.
The lucky ones reside with names, dates, a few yards
of overgrown weeds that admit this life is never truly ours.

We're what some call cheap, flashy, common, misplaced,
nothing you would want to bring home, unless placed
in a container and washed, kept under your bed, laced

with warnings, ridicule, and a clearly labeled disclaimer:
Pretend you are someone else. Don't admit you're the claimer
of the second-rate; instead, pretend you have worthy aims.

**Large Turquoise Nuggets with
Mother of Pearl 30"**

Red Christmas Bell with Crystals

No need for a holiday, we're always celebrating,
ready for someone to ring our bells, without a berating
somebody-else nearby who can't take the noise, rating

quiet with devout quality. All it takes is willpower
and we'll echo in your ears like church bells, our power
bridging sight and sound, have you saying *Amen* for hours.

It's okay to get all holy with us. We are, after all, *Christmas—*
miraculous in our own right. What body isn't, even Christ.
We all pretend he didn't want a scarlet piece of ass

somewhere along the way. I know, we're irreverent,
but that's to be expected when you live forever and
can't roll back the tombstone. You're left to rant

and rave like a lost disciple, a traitor, a proselyte
who's expired, who barely has the strength left to salute
the Mighty Father. So let us in the door. We'll light

your internal fires, leave you using glossolalia—
that's sexy talk for speaking in tongues, "glossa" and "laleo,"
Greek, meaning "the sound of language": *God is all, god is all.*

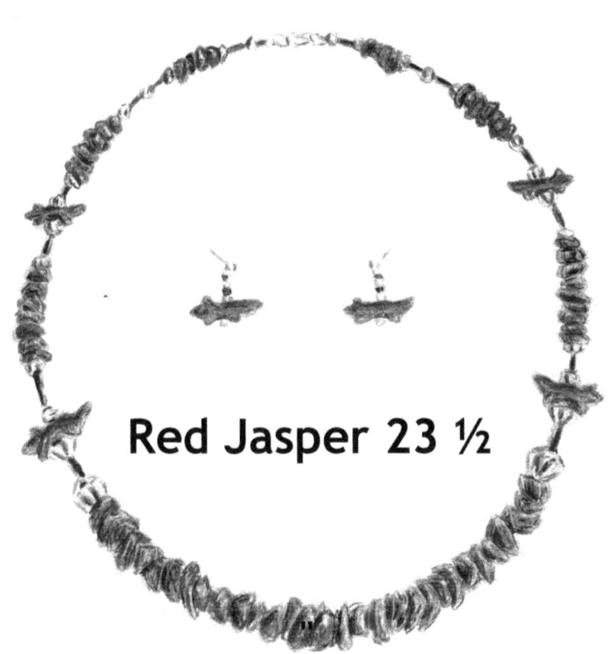

Toss out those vitamins! Forget the gym. Interested in restoring
your health? The Egyptian stone of endurance awaits you, storing
its potency and stamina in a rocky ruby-red speckled ring.

Wear us for rejuvenation or for a burst of youth, your libido
will thank you. We'll outlast pills, dr.'s visits, the highest bid—
or the strongest swimmer. We're that good at what we do.

We can't help spreading our news, the glow of our fertility
paints our cheeks a permanent blood-blush, hot until it
burns itself out: a forgotten fire, one once nurtured and lit.

Iron actually helps color our bodies, sharing its medicine
of veined love, protection, and concentration. It is in
our folds, our crevasses, our souls; it stirs us from within.

Don't be fooled by our siblings, Green or Yellow Jasper,
decorating the High Priests' breastplates, old school, as per
Biblical times. We're today's bomb, Red-hot, if not quite pure.

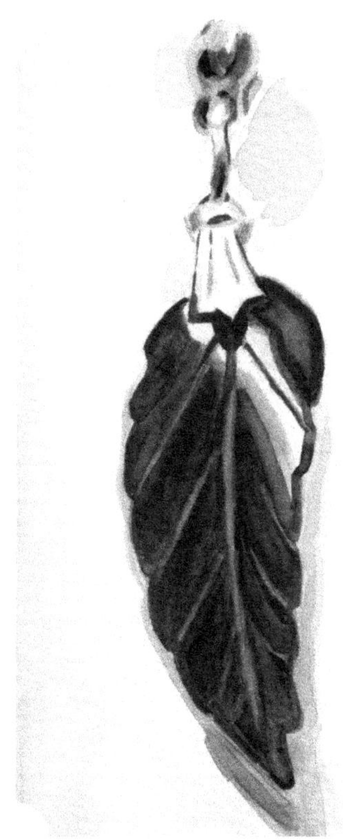 

Green Jade Leaf 1 5/8 " Dangle

Our story? Just two leaves dangling down, nature's clothing
since the world began, since Eve patented the fruit of body loathing.
That story? Well, you don't know the whole truth. The thing

is, Eve actually picked two apples that windless day, mistaking
them for shiny gems, treasures growing above ground, staking
her claim not on a famished gut, but self-reflection. Barely taking

a breath before they were in her hands, their crispy shimmer
cast a shiver she had never felt with Adam, though she loved him or
at least thought she did. Most of the time he was still her

main rib, unless, of course, she fell asleep and fantasized
about a larger man—one who could make mountains and sized
her up on a daily basis, leaving her, most days, a little blurry-eyed.

Milky Quartz with Black Crystals—
One of a Kind 20"

I wouldn't lie to you. I'm one of a kind, a sophisticated combination
of mammary fluid and rock, a patriotic girl just serving her nation,
fighting the enemy of daily life, lifting pressure by the ton

without even raising a shovel. Notice how I slowly enlarge, swelling
inch by inch, hardly noticeable if done gradually, my small orbs welling
between tan collarbones, multiplying and cloning themselves in

the air, before going back to their hiding spot, clasped together
and covered with hair—for without a lock I spill everywhere. (To get
your respect, I quote Rumi: *Close your Eyes, Fall in Love, Stay there.*)

Yellow Jade only 3 left

No, I'm not your grandmother's pearls, pulled out for church services;
I'm made of something different, composed for others' visual vices.
My yellow does not spell cowardice, but warm blessings. Simon says,

Put me on. Simon says, *Pretend you are an important sophisticated somebody.*
Simon says, *Don't forget my matching accessories; some bodies*
need some help. Pretend it's the first time as I wrap around your aging body.

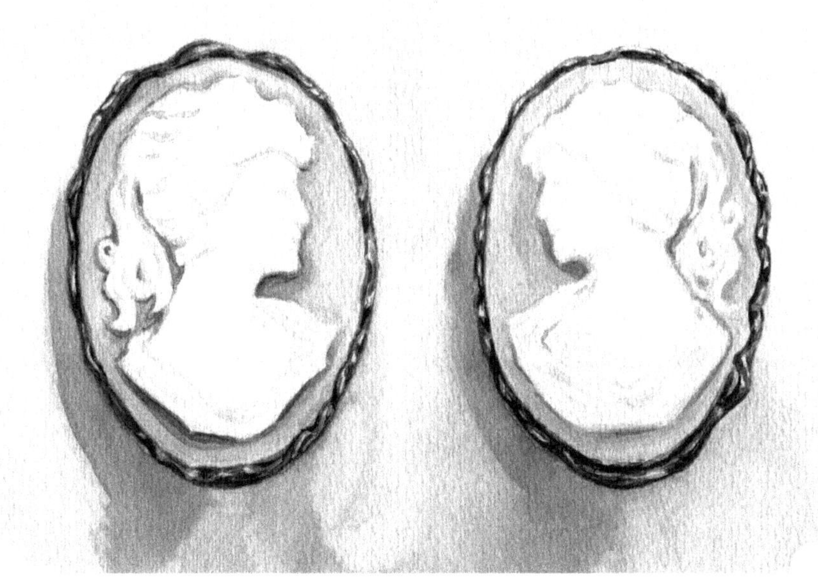

Blue Cameo on Silver-Plated Clips

Underneath it all, beneath the layers of gems and clothes, I'm a woman
who breathes, who smiles, who talks without words—my face, an omen
of coming storms and wars: the most beautiful plague ever carved by man.

Divine

Born Harris Glen Milstead on October 19, 1945, Divine was raised by a middle-class conservative family in the Baltimore suburb of Lutherville. It is difficult to feature Divine without the inclusion of his teenage friend and fellow collaborative artist, John Waters (also raised in Lutherville), who routinely cast Divine in his independent films as a character actor of notable bad taste.

Waters gave Milstead the name, "Divine," as well as the label, "the most beautiful woman in the world, almost." In tribute to their collaboration, the following series of poems utilize quotes from Waters as their choral refrains. Divine's counterculture, over-the-top drag persona created a cult following, which continues to this day. *People* magazine called him "Drag Queen of the Century" in 1988.

In the early 1980's Divine embarked on a short vocal side-career, in which he recorded disco tracks, primarily written by Bobby Orlando. The following series of poems utilizes the titles from ten of Divine's tracks, as well as contour interpretations of the album covers which housed those tracks. Divine died in his sleep from an enlarged heart on March 7, 1988 in a Los Angeles hotel, while waiting to film a cameo appearance on the sitcom *Married . . . with Children.*

TRACKS

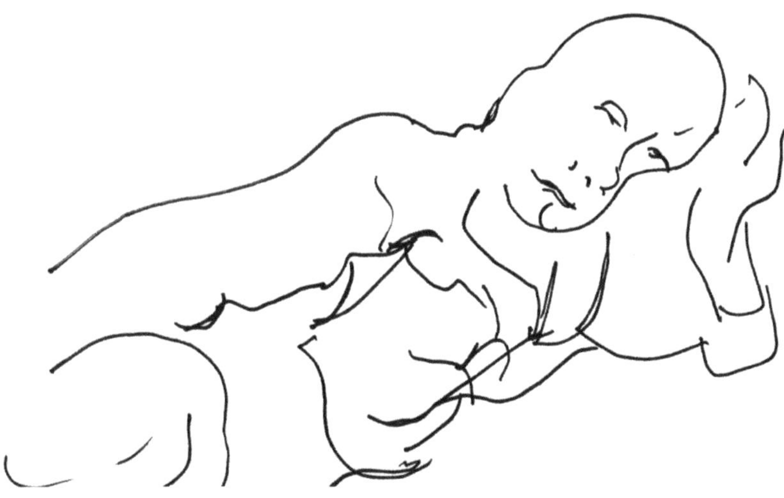

***Poetic Form:** *Divine's originality, pop-culture flair, and musical ambitions called for a lyric-driven contemporary form. Poet Afaa Michael Weaver's recent creation of "the bop" was a compelling fit. Weaver, raised in East Baltimore, invented the form at a summer Cave Canem retreat. "The Bop" establishes an argument, which is explored through three stanzas and a repeating refrain. The first stanza states the problem, the second stanza develops the problem, and the third stanza presents a resolution or an acknowledgment of a lack of resolution.*

***Artistic Medium:** *Black felt tip pen on paper. "Blind Contour" and "Semi-Blind Contour" drawings. "Blind contour" refers to drawing without looking at the paper, while the artist solely focuses on the contour lines of the subject. With "Semi-blind contour," the artist takes occasional brief glances at the paper during the drawing process. Contour line drawings' bold expressive qualities capture Divine's larger-than-life, outrageous personality.*

Female Trouble

I've got the teased hair, the penciled lips, the kiss
needed to launch at least one desperate ship.
I've got the winged eyes, the penciled brows—
perfect arches curved into the top of a heart,
ready to pounce on my new young Valentine.
What have I missed?

The most beautiful woman in the world, almost.

I've got the bust, double G's, delicious
in their stiff thrust through my sweaters,
ball gowns cinched so tight I flame out
into rolled glory: a bird, a mermaid, a siren
who beacons with a deep screeching voice.
I've got the shoes, huge open toes, painted claws
that click and cut, happy to wrap right around
a .22, ready to kill or love or both, at once.

The most beautiful woman in the world, almost.

Dangling diamonds, feather bracelets, bone pendants,
purses lined with fringe, animal prints, sequins,
sparkly panty-hose loose enough to let my gut
make its own debut and repeated cameos.
None of its matters, though, without my forced sneer,
sinister wink, pouty smile, or practiced pose. I am

the most beautiful woman in the world, almost.

Born to be Cheap

It takes refinement to be this cheap,
practice and care, the time to pick tacky
over boring, vulgar over banal and bleak.
It takes money to be this cheap—the slippery
slide of the credit card, a statement that
ends up in the same place each month: the trash.

An exercise in poor taste

It takes generosity to be this cheap,
and the need to share; without friends there
would be no need to care, to pick
the worst of the best or the best of the worst.
It takes class to be this cheap—
training, poise: you need lessons!
Not any ol' cheap will do—it's specialized,
tasteless, not found anywhere, or standardized.

An exercise in poor taste

This isn't something you can request.
It's a gift really, born of a time and place
long gone—a dirty storybook land located
between torn, over-read books and old maps,
between sweaty men and smoking ladies.
Go back further. You might be able to see it:

An exercise in poor taste

Native Love (Step by Step)

What's a moody boy from Lutherville supposed to do
when native love comes calling,
when he's done with split-levels and tractors,
Tupperware parties, and weekly trips to Murphy's Mart
when dad gets paid and Mom needs a new slip for church?
Why, wear it—of course, and show love tight in all its glory!

You don't wanna stay on your farm in Kansas forever.

There's a place past where the bus line ends and begins,
and if you take it both ways it might lead you
somewhere—downtown, uptown, in town or to some town
they say is your own town but could only be the place
people stop for gas and mean to leave, but don't.*
Instead, you find a few excuses, a job, gather bills,
and soon enough, start planning for your grave.
It's okay. I made it as far as L.A.

You don't wanna stay on your farm in Kansas forever.

The wizard awaits—in the bushes and the trees,
in high heels that dance until they bleed.
Dance with me. Yes, you. I'll take the lead.
The Hippo's gone, but we've still got the speed.
Hold my hand. Don't be scared. You can cry.
Feel the ferns tightening around your knees.

You don't wanna stay on your farm in Kansas forever.

* This line refers to the John Waters's quote: "It's as if every eccentric in the
South decided to move North, ran out of gas in Baltimore, and decided
to stay. No one moves here."

Shoot Your Shot

Love hurts, but so does heartburn and gas, liquid
bubbling up and out the pipe, hot like my hour-glass,
powdered and protected like Grandma's loose skin.
Love hurts, but so does a teased wig, the glue
against my scalp, the fake eyelashes that pull my lids
into two caterpillars caught in an angry web.

A face should jolt, not soothe.

There are some of us who have to hurt.
We can't feel ourselves, otherwise.
We prefer the iron to the ironing board,
the whip to whipped cream . . . well, maybe not.
We won't be happy until you make us crazy,
smother us with your attention, tell us
we rock your world, at least for today.
It's a good hurt. A stray bullet that lasts

A face should jolt, not soothe.

much longer than a typical surface wound.
Maybe that's why we run into the middle of fights,
without warning or protection or plans.
Love always finds us there, in all that chaos,
drapes its liquid arms around us and does not hide
or apologize or excuse itself for coming into being.

A face should jolt, not soothe.

Love Reaction

No need for a microscope, I arrive in full-focus—
magnified to optimum view, too big for any slide
or formula or equation, my body only loyal
to polyester and pursed lips: a wrecked U.F.O.
glowing silver and black, radiating its metallic
parts across a sheer and snug, black nylon sky.

To me, beauty is looks you can never forget.

Who said space was tasteful, high society, or
a cosmic club that only accepts understated matter?
There are plenty of constellations that don't fit that mold,
who light so bright they, alone, trick black holes.
No, you can't find me by way of the Hubble.
I don't stay in one spot long enough to be plotted
or marked with solid, sterile instruments.
I'll explode before you can catch me.

To me, beauty is looks you can never forget.

Forget the stars, baby, I'm the trail that keeps
on trailing, particles that span across time and space,
a laboratory where measurements need not
be measured in clean precision or mock trials.
Some say you need sunglasses to view my eclipse;
I say take them off—burn those corneas—I won't last!

To me, beauty is looks you can never forget.

T Shirts and Tight Blue Jeans

I know it's been quite a few years since you've
felt that old friend against your chest—
that touch of fresh decal between your pecs.
It still holds the smell of the shop: backstage passes,
bus tours, drunken groupies, and the uncanny hope
you've almost made it there, but not quite.

Without obsession, life is nothing.

I know it's been fifteen minutes since you've
last tugged up your jeans, felt that old friend
slide into its spot, pulled the waist down
so that you could breathe without holding your breath.
I know you're not young anymore,
but you can still see it that way, see yourself
in a T-shirt and tight blue jeans—
a casual man any man would love.

Without obsession, life is nothing.

If it wasn't for T-shirts and tight blue jeans,
we would all be kings or Presidents or cops.
How could we walk down the street and whistle
without cotton or denim or zippers?
Some collect cards or thimbles or spoons;
I stick to wardrobes and muscles.

Without obsession, life is nothing.

Without obsession, life is nothing.

You Think You're a Man

But think again, sweetheart, no man would
look like you, would sing like you, would
promise so much and give so little.
It takes a real man to keep things real.
You're nothing but a phony, an imposter,
a man dressed up like a man dressed up like a man.

If you go home with somebody and they don't have books,
don't fuck them.

At least that's what my momma said,
at least until her man beat her with a belt
and a little white church that cut just as hard.
I should have guessed your shelves
would be stacked with liquor instead of Keats,
snow globes instead of Wilde, old pictures
of a boy who looked strong enough
to make it all the way to the finish line.

If you go home with somebody and they don't have books,
don't fuck them.

I learned the hard way. Empty shelves
are empty arms. Empty arms are nothing
but empty shelves. There's no use even trying.
You think you're a man. You think you're a man.
You think you're a man? You think?
You're a man? What do you think?

If you go home with somebody and they don't have books,
don't fuck them.

I'm So Beautiful

Beauty is in the eye of the beholder, at least that's
what they say. Who say? You say?
Why *they*, of course, the same *they* who paint
inside the lines, who make lists of the requirements
one must check off to be officially . . . beautiful.
That's okay. I'm beautiful on the inside.

Ever feel like killing somebody
just to see if you could get away with it?

Today's beauty consists of ten new stretch marks,
eye boogers from a late night, and a rough
and scratchy throat. Today's beauty is full-out
heat, packing rhythmic moves like a human shoot-out,
legs shuffling, chafing, blistering themselves.
You'll need a new clipboard and page to capture
this beauty, one that lists laughter, tears, your
hand covering your eyes because it is that beautiful.

Ever feel like killing somebody
just to see if you could get away with it?

The skin rubs away easier than you might imagine,
the eyes pop out like little allergic grapes.
You don't need a knife, maybe just a few incisions.
Stay steady and consistent in your work.
The heart is already dying, expired and swollen,
so you just need to wait, just a little while.

Ever feel like killing somebody
just to see if you could get away with it?

Hard Magic

First, create a base: a creamy broth of misfits,
those with crooked teeth, chicken skin arms,
square pegs who refuse round holes,
or the ornery ones who simply won't obey.
Make it lukewarm, hot enough to entice, but not scold.
It helps if you let it boil first, before your stir.

*Who would have thought a good little girl like you
could destroy my beautiful wickedness?**

Remember to add some parental quotes,
You will not and *we did not raise you*
are recommended, although most will suffice.
Throw in some smokes and beers, maybe a joint
or two, and any other unsavory characters
who happen to be strolling by that day.
Don't forget a decent amount of foul language,
espccially the ones that make teachers squirm.

*Who would have thought a good little girl like you
could destroy my beautiful wickedness?*

Last, create a glaze: a sweet drizzle of *Watch me*,
and watch it slowly slide down the sides
of your cauldron. You can test-taste it first,
if you like, but most prefer to just administer.
I recommend a nightly dosage, starting at age thirteen.
but some swear twelve, or even eleven.

*Who would have thought a good little girl like you
could destroy my beautiful wickedness?*

Full Waters's quote: "When they throw water on the witch, she says, 'Who would have thought a good little girl like you could destroy my beautiful wickedness?' That line inspired my life. I sometimes say it to myself before I go to sleep, like a prayer."

Hey You!

Take a few minutes to stop and stare.
I'm the real deal, the raw feeling
of what you keep in check, at least in public.
This show is on the house, just for you,
but, please, no pictures unless you swear
to show them to everyone, everywhere!

*I pride myself on the fact that my work
has no socially redeeming value.*

I know I'm a lot to handle, a lot
to take in, to keep even halfway contained,
like a bad rash or a dark, hairy mole.
Even with your best effort, you can't help it—
your eyes give you away every time.
They can't run or hide or pretend.
Remember what your mother said:
Don't stare. Don't make a scene. Be polite.

*I pride myself on the fact that my work
has no socially redeeming value.*

Is it boring, to look like everyone else?
Is it lonely, to have to get approval
before you decide what you want to say?
From where I stand, the bars surround you,
not me. You stand there, so very worried.
I stare. I make a scene. I'm impolite.

*I pride myself on the fact that my work
has no socially redeeming value.*

Axl Rotten

Axl Rotten was born Brian Knighton on April 21, 1971 in Fell's Point, Maryland. Rotten attended Southern High School through the 11th grade, at which time he dropped out to pursue a professional wrestling career. Trained by "Bad Boy" Ricky Lawless (who trained some of the country's top wrestlers in his gym on the corner of North Avenue and Harford Road before he was murdered by his girlfriend's husband in 1988), Rotten created his ring name by combining the names of Axl Rose and Johnny Rotten. Rotten and his ring "brother," Ian Rotten (John Williams), formed The Bad Breed tag team during the 1992 Global Wrestling Federation promotion.

The "brothers" were brief winners of the Global Wrestling Federation Championship title in 1993 and continued to perform globally and nationally for the next decade. Years of back trauma resulted in severe spinal injuries which left Rotten unable to walk in 2014, pending serious back surgeries and intensive rehabilitation.

Rotten also suffered from substance abuse for much of his life. He died of a heroin overdose at a McDonald's in Linthicum, Maryland on February 4, 2016. The following illustrations are based on photographs and posts obtained from Rotten's Facebook and Twitter pages three months after his death.

Ink

***Poetic Form:** *Inspired by Afaa Michael Weaver's original poetry form, "the bop," a new poetry form was created for this collection to capture Axl Rotten's photographs and posts: "the bay." Reflecting the bright and dark sides of Baltimore's watersheds, "the bay" mirrors the distorted duality of surface versus below-surface representations of an identical rhyming stanza structure (ABABAB) with an inner repeating couplet (the meeting point of two realities).*

***Artistic Medium:** *Black watercolor paint on watercolor paper. Using different style brushes with varying viscosities of paint creates layers of textures which give a feeling of ink and grittiness to represent Rotten's life, his personality, and his tattoos.*

"A year ago 2day I was in the hospital unable to walk.
I'm at the beach enjoying the sun. #recovery #faith"
-Axl Rotten

#Recovery

One day I woke up, unable to walk.
You've got a chance, the docs said,
but you'll need to do more than talk.
You had already left me for dead,
forgotten the man with the mohawk,
the man who fought and always bled.

Surprise! I'm still here.
Surprise! I'm still here.

It was real. Real blood. I always bled
so it could run down my mohawk,
so you, too, knew you were not dead.
That's why most came to see me, talked
shit, and came back. That's all unsaid.
Today I woke up, finally able to walk.

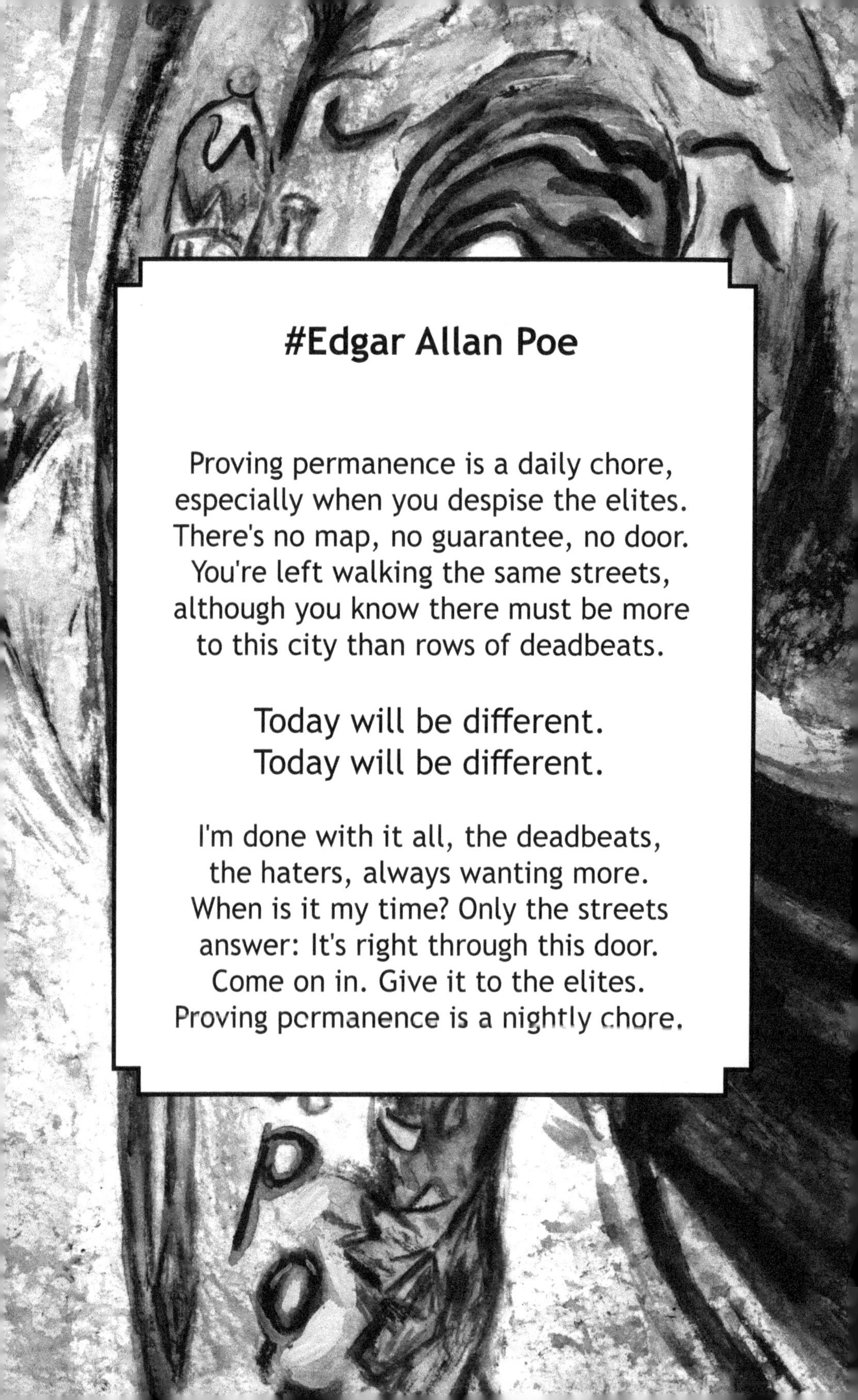

#Edgar Allan Poe

Proving permanence is a daily chore,
especially when you despise the elites.
There's no map, no guarantee, no door.
You're left walking the same streets,
although you know there must be more
to this city than rows of deadbeats.

Today will be different.
Today will be different.

I'm done with it all, the deadbeats,
the haters, always wanting more.
When is it my time? Only the streets
answer: It's right through this door.
Come on in. Give it to the elites.
Proving permanence is a nightly chore.

"Just to prove my love for #Baltimore and #EdgarAllanPoe
this is my #tattoo that is on my left forearm.
#charm city Thanks for #DeVilleInk"
-Axl Rotten

"Another doctors appointment is in the books
trying to get better!
#AxlStrong #recovery"
-Axl Rotten

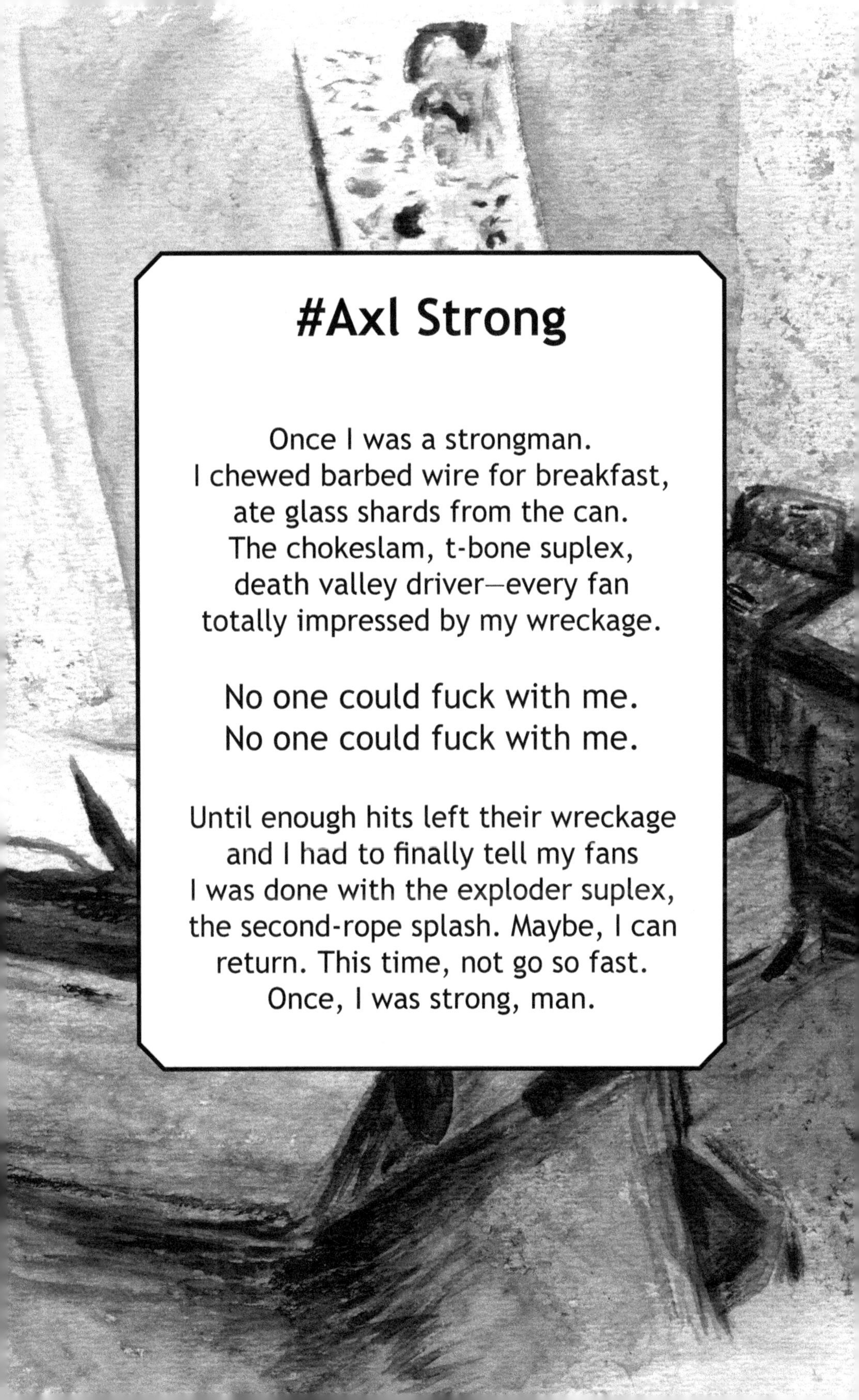

#Axl Strong

Once I was a strongman.
I chewed barbed wire for breakfast,
ate glass shards from the can.
The chokeslam, t-bone suplex,
death valley driver—every fan
totally impressed by my wreckage.

No one could fuck with me.
No one could fuck with me.

Until enough hits left their wreckage
and I had to finally tell my fans
I was done with the exploder suplex,
the second-rope splash. Maybe, I can
return. This time, not go so fast.
Once, I was strong, man.

#KISSARMY

Only one other man has come close
in his badassness, his body tricks
found inside his own mouth, a pro's
lingual tribute to the extreme fix.
Meet the Demon: performing shows,
devouring women, in spite of the risks.

Fans like their heroes simple.*
Fans like their heroes simple:

Just a tongue, some scars. Without risks
it's just the Brian Knighton show.
Without any ink, no one could fix
a broken system—the colorful prose
needed to believe life's more than tricks,
to remember the men who come close.

* Quote by Gene Simmons

"Check out my Badass @genesimmons #tattoo @KISSOnline #KISS #KISSARMY"
-Axl Rotten

"DO NOT be fooled... A moment of brief wealth is
NO substitute for leading a rich life. - #AxlsAdvice #truth"
-Axl Rotten

#AxlsAdvice

There is nothing like the smell of money,
the crisp edges, ink hardened into paper form.
Center stage: old men dressed up, the history,
make-up, and powder of those already born
into view, into memory, into a country
where wealth and power rule. I warn:

Do NOT be fooled . . .
Do NOT be fooled . . .

it only takes one wrong move to warm
up to the thought that you own this country,
to think you are more, when you were just born
for a moment within its edited history,
the quick pic of a lost life, a living form
who was nothing, without the money.

#Dogma

Believe that love is the other side of hate:
the self that cannot stay quiet or release
itself from the burden of its own weight.
Believe that those who cannot please
are simply aiming for a different fate
than the usual—that of death and disease.

Until death do you part.
Until death do you part.

Believe that you can take disease
and pile-drive it into oblivion; Fate
might not even recognize you, pleased
with another young man who couldn't wait.
Believe that there is ease in release.
Believe that Love is the other half of Hate.

"My old school @marilynmanson #tattoo from the "Portrait of an American Family" album. It changed my life. #dogma"
- Axl Rotten

"This is what I'm doing. Back on the #scifit at #physicaltherapy #cardio #rehab #gym #NeverGiveup"
-Axl Rotten

#Rehab

No one warns you that "after" begins
before "before" ends. No one tells you
the day or the place when your limbs
decide they're done. Like that, your new
life unfolds: you're one of many has-beens,
the man who once gave the devil his due.

No one knows how hard it is to walk.
No one knows how hard it is to walk.

Unless they, too, woke up one day, overdue
on borrowed time, yesterday's might-have-beens.
Imagine what it's like: finding a new
body lying in front of you, numb limbs
that don't listen, that only scream, You—
we warned you. Now, the real work begins!

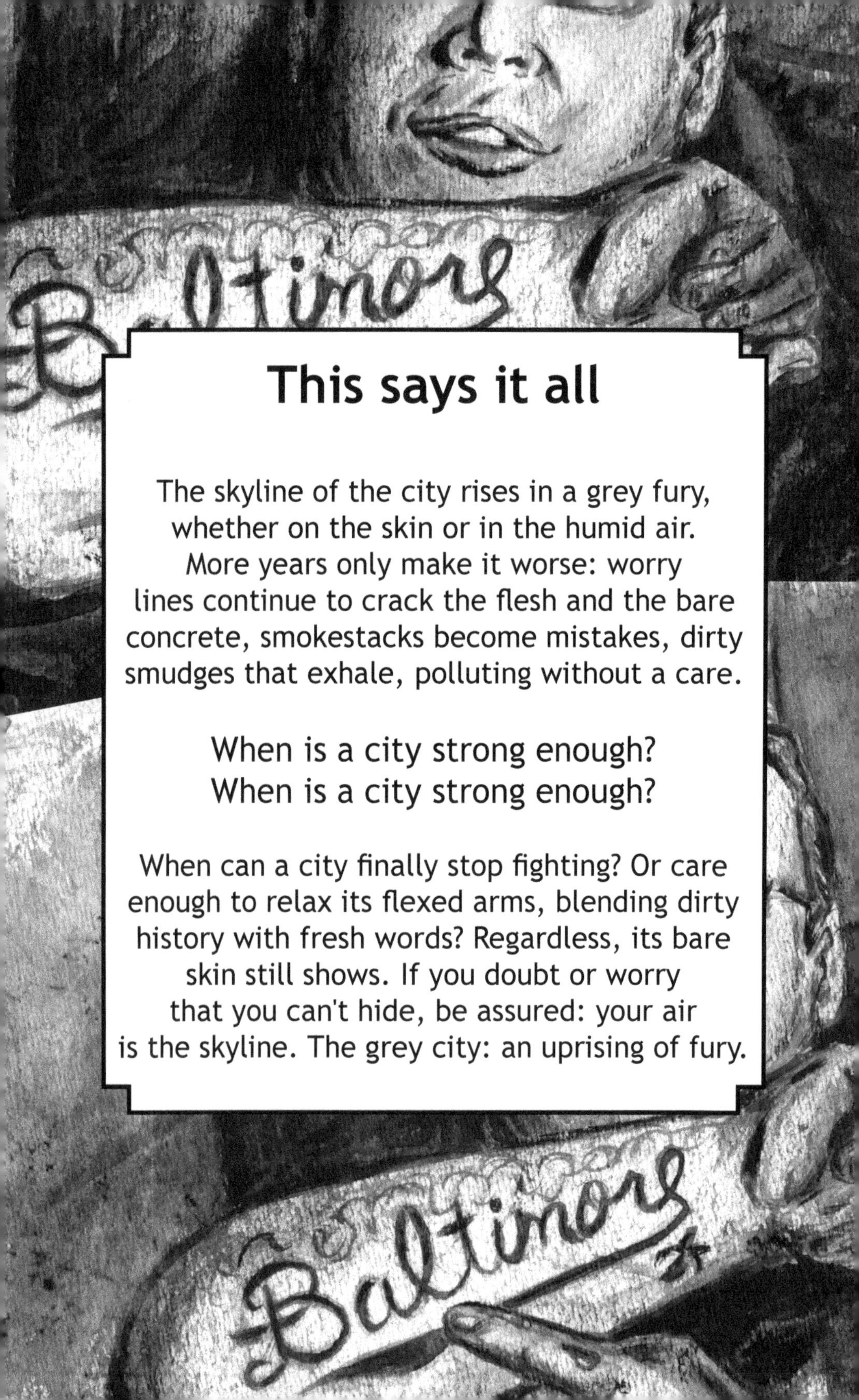

This says it all

The skyline of the city rises in a grey fury,
whether on the skin or in the humid air.
More years only make it worse: worry
lines continue to crack the flesh and the bare
concrete, smokestacks become mistakes, dirty
smudges that exhale, polluting without a care.

When is a city strong enough?
When is a city strong enough?

When can a city finally stop fighting? Or care
enough to relax its flexed arms, blending dirty
history with fresh words? Regardless, its bare
skin still shows. If you doubt or worry
that you can't hide, be assured: your air
is the skyline. The grey city: an uprising of fury.

"@HOCKYHOOLIGAN7 this says it all"
-Axl Rotten

"I think its funny how motherfuckers wrote me off and
I'm still standing. I refused to go down. I will survive."
-Axl Rotten

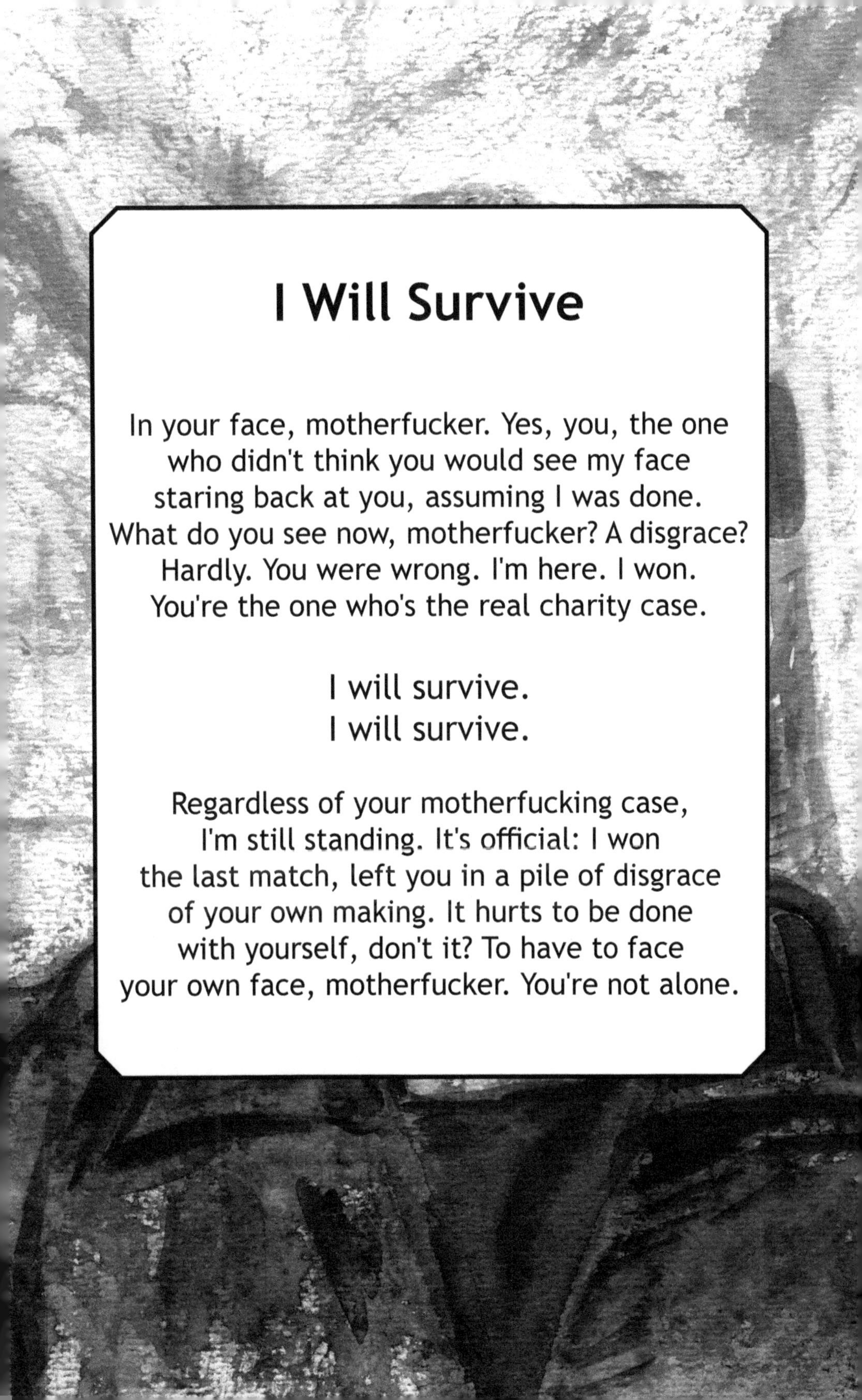

I Will Survive

In your face, motherfucker. Yes, you, the one
who didn't think you would see my face
staring back at you, assuming I was done.
What do you see now, motherfucker? A disgrace?
Hardly. You were wrong. I'm here. I won.
You're the one who's the real charity case.

I will survive.
I will survive.

Regardless of your motherfucking case,
I'm still standing. It's official: I won
the last match, left you in a pile of disgrace
of your own making. It hurts to be done
with yourself, don't it? To have to face
your own face, motherfucker. You're not alone.

#Pain

From my view, it's PAIN, four letters which spell
my new and old motto: the hits I had to give,
the shit that drove me to bleed, to sell
myself as the Bad Breed who couldn't live
with or without myself. Being well
doesn't mean you aren't sick, or alive.

You will find out there is only 1 way. My away!*

You will find out there is only 1 way. My away!

From your view, it could be WEED—a life
caught up in smoke and mirrors, well-
lit until the high ended and you had to live
on in spite of lost dreams. Or, perhaps, sell
yourself for that one and final chance to give
a show which spells READ: A fist and four letters.

*Axl Rotten's last tweet, posted on February 4, 2016 #Axls Truth

Henrietta Lacks

Henrietta Lacks was born Loretta Pleasant on August 1, 1920 in Roanoke, Virginia. When Lacks was four years old, her mother died and she was sent to live in Clover, Virginia on a tobacco farm with her grandfather, where she shared a room with her nine-year-old cousin and future husband, David "Day" Lacks. In 1941, a relative persuaded the Lacks family to move to Baltimore so that Day could work at Bethlehem Steel. The family purchased a house in Turner Station, which is now a part of Dundalk. In January of 1951, Lacks was diagnosed with cervical cancer in the segregated ward of Johns Hopkins Hospital. Cancerous tissue samples from her cervix were taken without her or her family's knowledge and were soon discovered to reproduce and live for a much longer period than typical cells.

The cells were mass produced and marketed for biomedical research, contributing to many major scientific breakthroughs and research, such as the polio vaccine and AIDS and cancer research. Since the 1950s, scientists have grown 20 tons of HeLa cells, but Lacks's family did not find out about the HeLa cells until the end of the century. Rebecca Skloot's 2010 book, *The Immortal Life of Henrietta Lacks*, documents the history of Lacks, the Lacks family, and the HeLa cells, including the various vessels which have carried Lacks's cells since 1951.

The Vessels

Poetic Form: Various forms were selected to tell the stories of the various vessels which carried the HeLa cells. Like the global (and beyond) journey of the cells, the following forms originated from all parts of the world during a range of literary time periods. While beginning in Baltimore, the side-show ends in a much larger town, one known by the name of Humanity.

Artistic Medium: Ink and technical pens on watercolor paper. An experimental approach was chosen to represent the scientific experiments related to the study of Lacks's cells and the spread of her cancer. Pen and ink drawings with ink strategically blown on the paper were used to serve this purpose.

Poetic Forms INDEX for 'The Vessels'

1) The Tumor, Turner Station, Baltimore

*Poetic Form: **Pantoum**

Originally a fifteenth-century Malaysian folk song form, the pantoum is composed of four-line stanzas in which the second and fourth lines of each stanza serve as the first and third lines of the next stanza. The last line of the poem, then, is also the first line of the poem.

2) The Test Tube, Johns Hopkins Hospital, Baltimore

*Poetic Form: **Rondeau**

Born as a lyric form in thirteenth-century France, the rondeau is composed of fifteen lines, organized into three stanzas: a quintet, quatrain, and sestet, with each line containing eight to ten syllables. The first few words of the first line of the first stanza, the rentrement, recurs as the final line of the second and third stanzas. The rhyme pattern is aabba/aabR/aabbaR (R being the refrain).

3) The Incubator, Johns Hopkins Hospital, Baltimore

*Poetic Form: **Haiku**

The haiku, short introductory verse which broke away from the longer renga form in sixteenth-century Japan, is a three-line poem with seventeen syllables, written in a 5/7/5 syllable count, which usually explores elements of nature.

4) The Postmaster's Hands, P.O. Main Branch, Baltimore

*Poetic form: **Sestina**

The sestina form is attributed to the Provencal Troubadours of the 12th century. It contains five six-line stanzas and an ending three-line stanza (envoi). Each line ends with a repeating word, as follows: ABCDEF/ FAEBDC/ CFDABE/ ECBFAD/ DEACFB/ BDFECA/ECA or ACE (with BDF also embedded).

5) The Pocket, at 5,000 feet above sea level

*Poetic form: **Doha**

The doha is a form composed of rhyming couplets originally found in Urdu and Hindi poetry dating back to the sixth century. Each line is made up of 24 syllables, divided into two phrases of thirteen and eleven syllables.

6) The Cargo Hold, en route to Texas

*Poetic Form: **Ballade**

A fourteenth and fifteenth-century French form, the ballade contains three main stanzas with an identical rhyme scheme, usually 'ababbcbC ababbcbC ababbcbC, followed by an envoi: bcbC, (C being the refrain).

7) The Saddlebag, the mountains in Chile

*Poetic form: **Villanelle**

The villanelle is a Renaissance-based Italian and Spanish song: a nineteen-line poem composed of five tercets followed by a quatrain. The first and third lines of the opening tercet are repeated alternately in the last lines of the succeeding stanzas; then in the final stanza, the refrain serves as the poem's two concluding lines. Using capitals for the refrains and lowercase letters for the rhymes, the form follows: A1 b A2 / a b A1 / a b A2 / a b A1 / a b A2 / a b A1 A2.

8) The Discoverer XVIII Satellite, Outer Space

*Poetic form: **Eintou**

The eintou is an African American poetry form consisting of seven lines with a total of 32 syllables or words. The term eintou is West African for "pearl," as in pearls of wisdom. The form is divided into seven lines, with the following syllable or word counts: 2/4/6/8/6/4/2.

9) The Unmarked Grave, Clover, Virginia

*Poetic Form: **Burmese Climbing Rhyme**

The Burmese climbing rhyme form is composed of a repeated sequence of three internally rhymed lines, consisting of four syllables each. In English versions, words are often used in place of syllables. There are several variations of Burmese climbing rhymes, which date back centuries. In this version, the rhyme moves from the fourth word, to the third word, to the second word, whereas a new rhyme begins to "climb" through the poem until reaching a conclusion.

10) The Woman, Everywhere

*Poetic form: **Ode**

Popularized by the Greeks and later, the Romantic poets, the ode uses a regular, recurrent stanza pattern to address a formal event, a person, or a thing not present. The Horatian ode is utilized here, which is more informal than other ode variations, such as the Pindaric and Irregular.

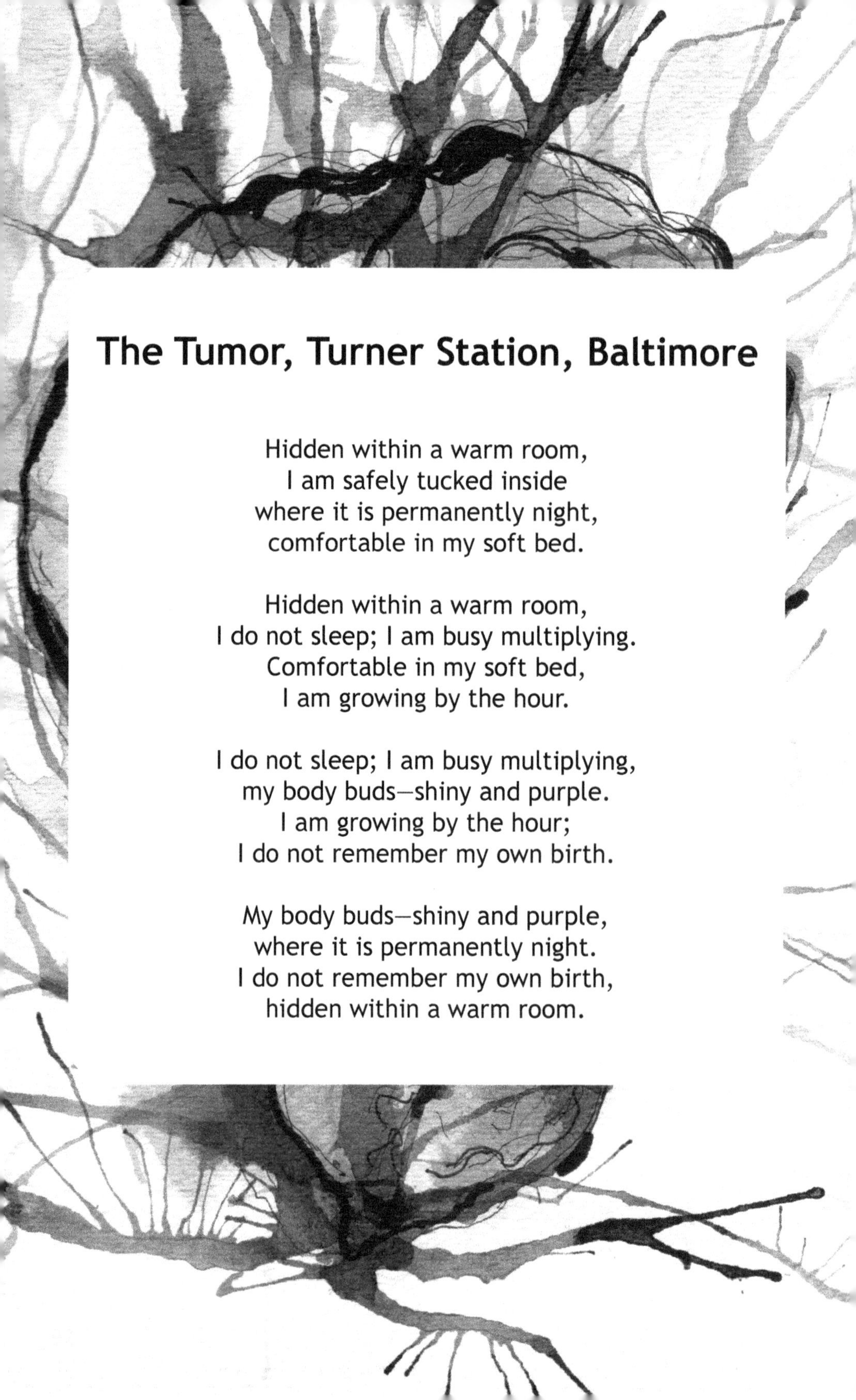

The Tumor, Turner Station, Baltimore

Hidden within a warm room,
I am safely tucked inside
where it is permanently night,
comfortable in my soft bed.

Hidden within a warm room,
I do not sleep; I am busy multiplying.
Comfortable in my soft bed,
I am growing by the hour.

I do not sleep; I am busy multiplying,
my body buds—shiny and purple.
I am growing by the hour;
I do not remember my own birth.

My body buds—shiny and purple,
where it is permanently night.
I do not remember my own birth,
hidden within a warm room.

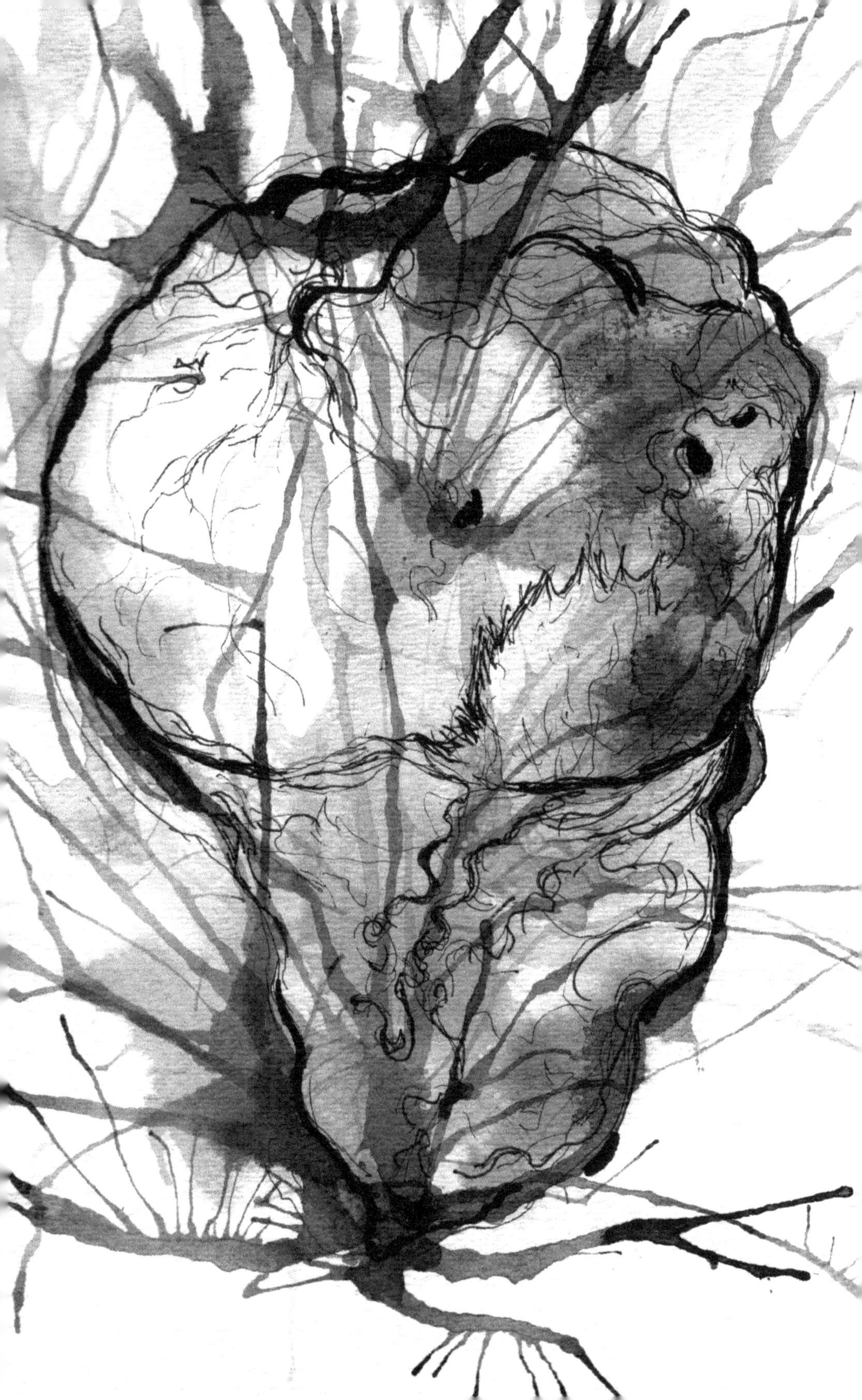

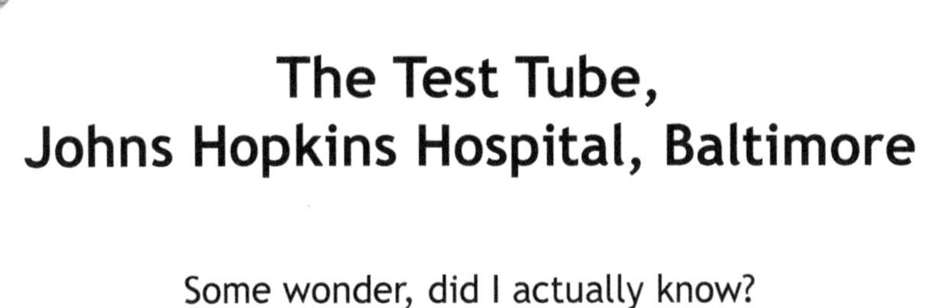

The Test Tube,
Johns Hopkins Hospital, Baltimore

Some wonder, did I actually know?
How could I? Most cells tend to grow
in silence. They usually do not speak.
They do not ask, or plead, or seek
permission. They are often very slow

to reveal their plans. They remain low
on the radar; an underground show.
Most times, they are fragile and weak.
Some wonder.

Yet, these cells could somehow outgrow
themselves in seconds—an indigo
colony—formed by a technique
that was completely new and unique:
to live immortal, to foreshadow
some wonder.

The Incubator,
Johns Hopkins Hospital, Baltimore

inside me—a world
a woman   an unpaid find
grow . . . grow . . . grow . . . grow . . . grow

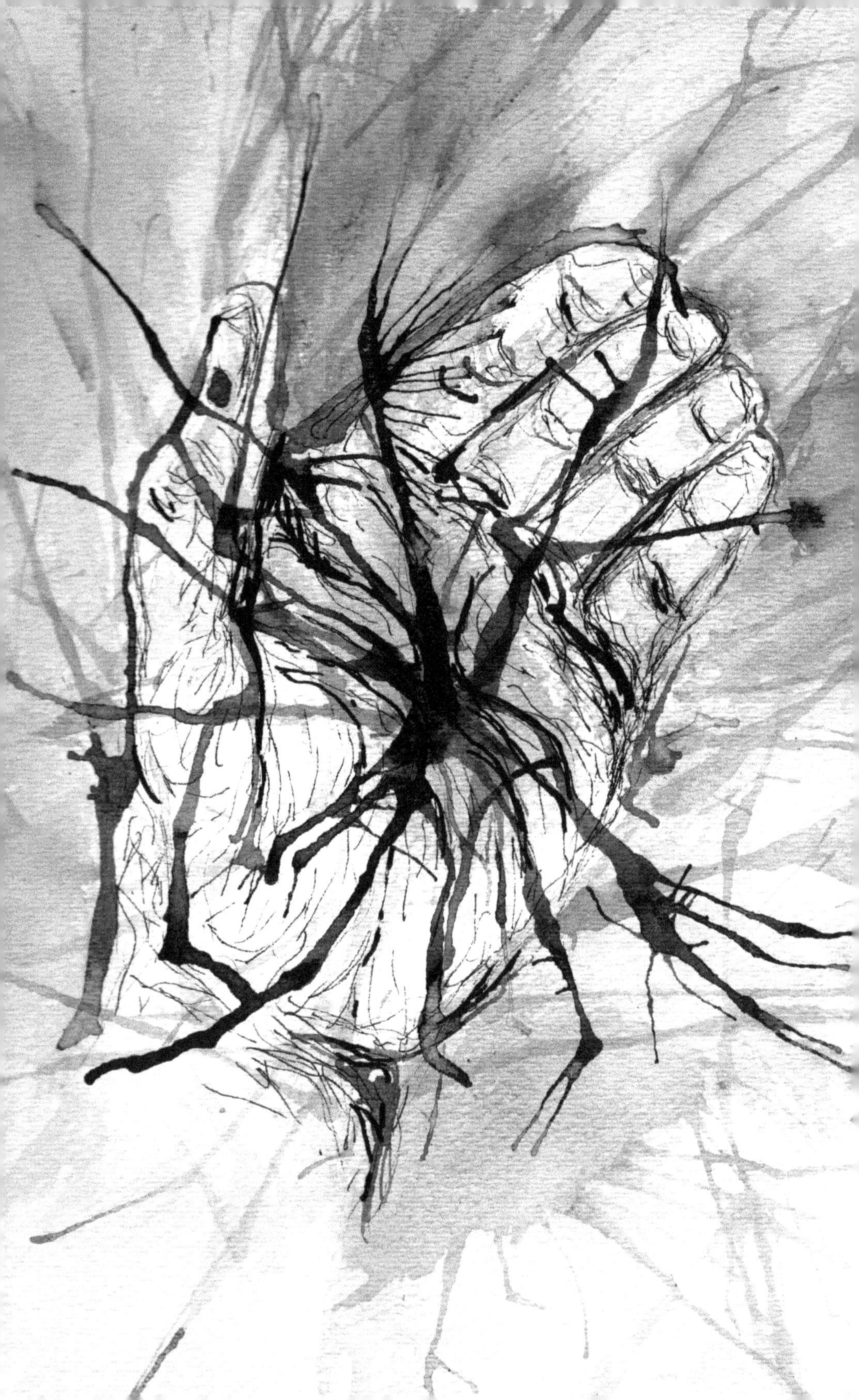

The Postmaster's Hands,
P.O. Main Branch, Baltimore

The packages are now just a blur—
a long strand of beige paper,
never-ending addresses and names
scrolling, continuing to unroll.
Day after day after day after day:
just more of the same.

At the beginning, the same
moves meant work, meant a blur
of hours, a check on Friday.
The feeling of all that paper
was only the job, the unrolling
of pride—a new title and name.

Then, I suddenly couldn't name
the day of the week, the same
motions were too similar to unroll
from another. My fingers blurred
into one finger, calloused like paper-
mache, getting harder each day.

So there is no way that today,
William Scherer would be a name
different from any other on paper,
Research Lab is listed the same
as Grandfather's house, or the blur
of a college, waiting to enroll.

It would be silly, to unroll
one life from another, one long day
from the next. Stopping the blur
of the line, just for one name
is madness. Better to keep the same
letters, formulas, paper.

Tell yourself that, or the papers
will speak to you, beg you to unroll
their contents, tell you that same
story you heard back in the day
you were a person without a name—
another abnormality in the blur.

Keep it going. Ignore the papers:
human packages blurring into one name,
one uneventful day, unrolling the same.

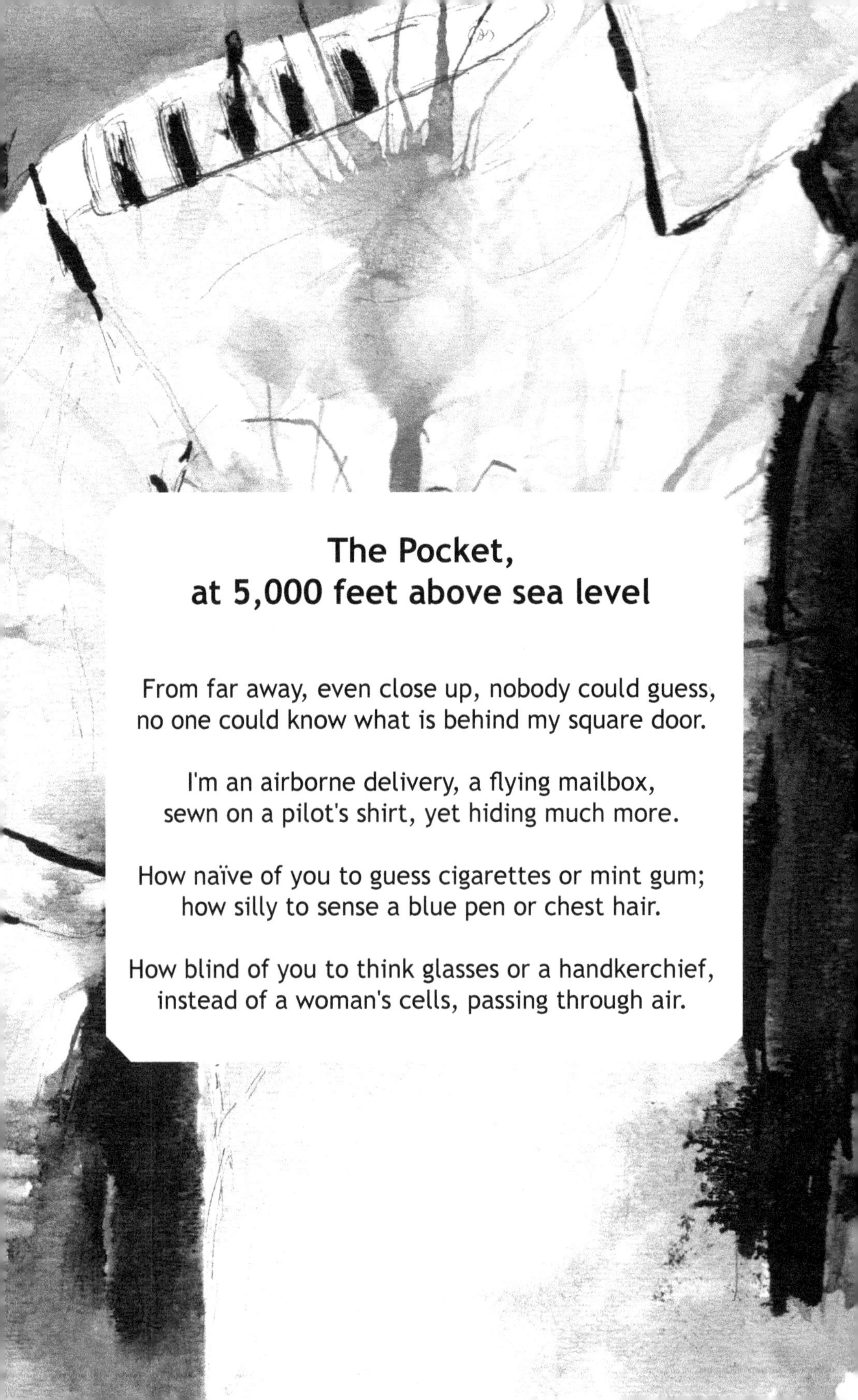

The Pocket,
at 5,000 feet above sea level

From far away, even close up, nobody could guess,
no one could know what is behind my square door.

I'm an airborne delivery, a flying mailbox,
sewn on a pilot's shirt, yet hiding much more.

How naïve of you to guess cigarettes or mint gum;
how silly to sense a blue pen or chest hair.

How blind of you to think glasses or a handkerchief,
instead of a woman's cells, passing through air.

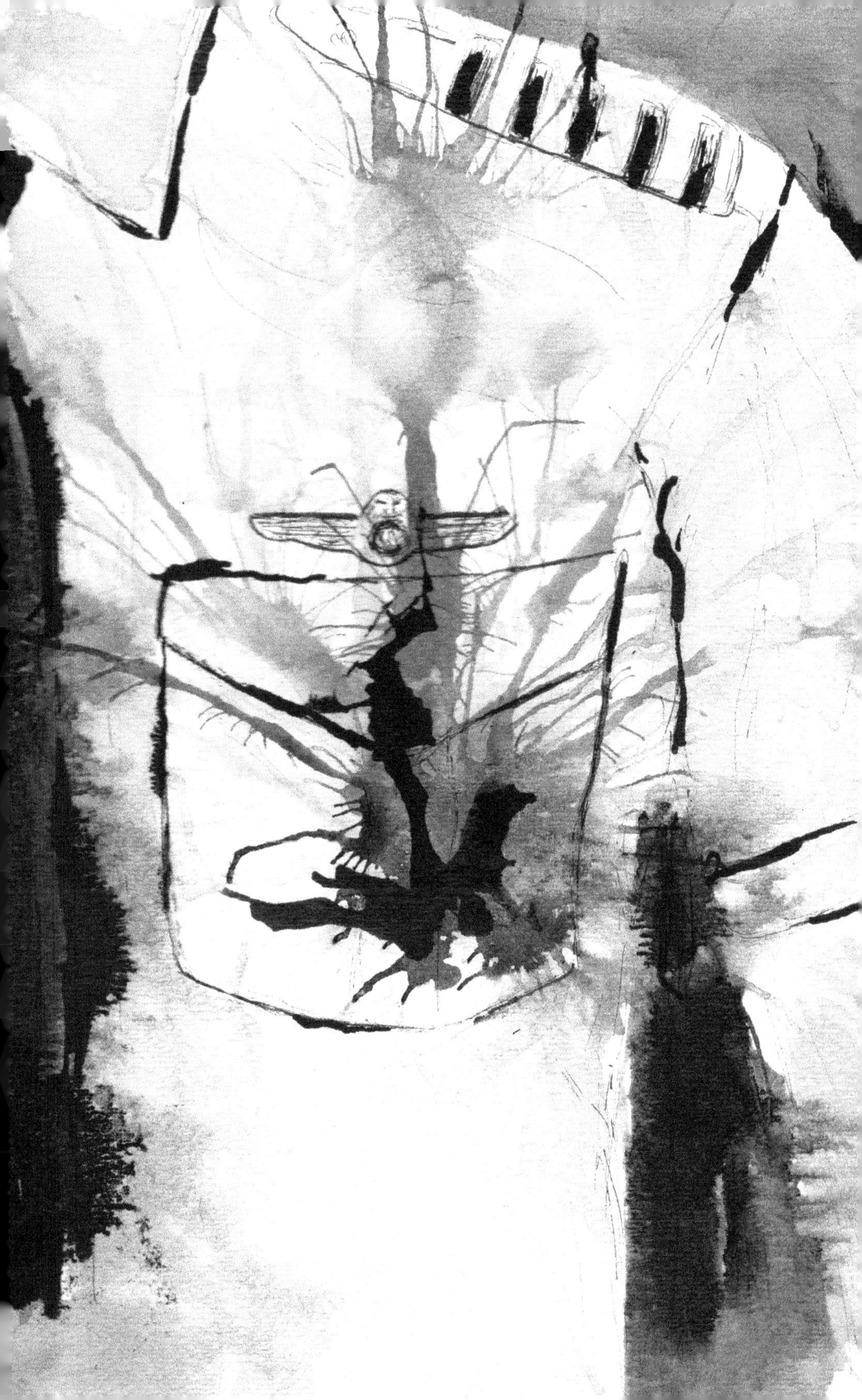

FRAGILE

The Cargo Hold, en route to Texas

My hard belly is packed tight
with children—bruised steel
bodies stacked in rows, fighting
to reach the top, to feel
what it is to win, to steal
others' air for one's own breath.
It's a child's game, only real,
played from birth until death.

Right now, a child hides, right
beside her siblings, kneeling
behind the others, barely in sight.
She is named FRAGILE—an appeal
for gentility, a handwritten ink seal
advertising the extent and breadth
of breakability, her inability to heal,
played from birth until death.

I worry it is too cold; she might
not make it, after being sealed
into custom ice blocks, then lightly
placed into saw dust. She reveals
nothing unusual, only the appeal
for care, for notice, for the depth
to realize she is not a business deal,
played from birth until death.

Hang tight, baby, someone will wheel
you out soon, even if after your death.
You will transcend this immortal ordeal,
replayed from birth until death.

The Saddlebag, the mountains in Chile

Each time, I wonder what it will be like to see
the sky up-close, to taste it. Move along.
Today, test tubes, tomorrow—corn and tea.

I wonder if we will reach an end. I doubt if we
will ever stop moving. Perhaps, I am wrong.
Underneath, hooves crunch, soothing me.

2 more miles, then 1 more past the last tree.
Hold on. This trip is temporary, and lifelong.
Today, test tubes, tomorrow—corn and tea.
Underneath, hooves crunch, soothing me.

The Discoverer XVIII Satellite,
Outer Space

The weight
of no weight weighs
heavier than you know;
no stops, breaks or needed pauses—
the weight will keep growing,
mercilessly:
no bounds.

The
Unmarked
Grave,

Clover, Virginia

I am here, though
not here, so hidden
that no existing sign,
word, or line can
truly define my contents.
Only a reference to
others presents my place—
an unmarked space, unsolved
cold case: invisible trace.

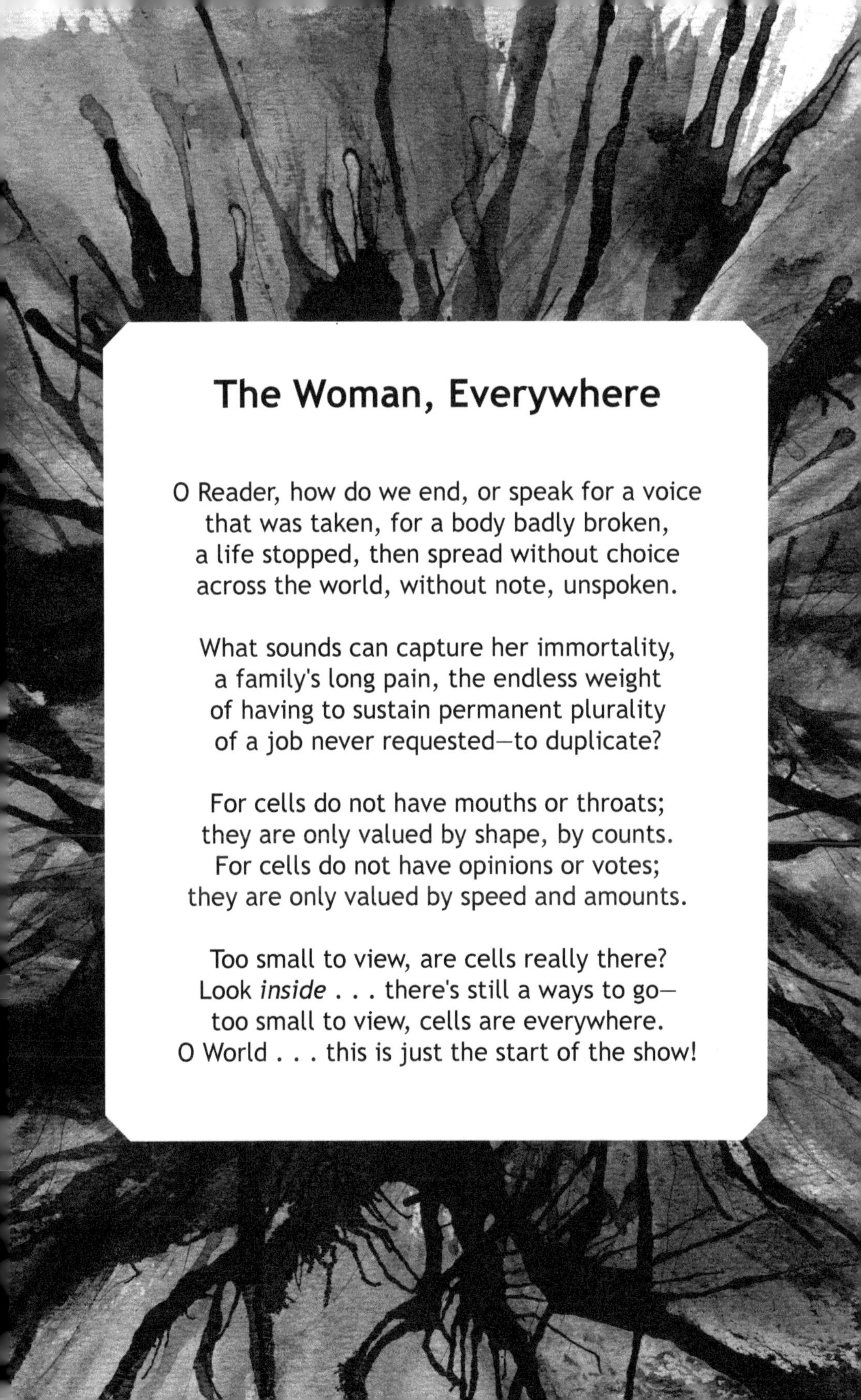

The Woman, Everywhere

O Reader, how do we end, or speak for a voice
that was taken, for a body badly broken,
a life stopped, then spread without choice
across the world, without note, unspoken.

What sounds can capture her immortality,
a family's long pain, the endless weight
of having to sustain permanent plurality
of a job never requested—to duplicate?

For cells do not have mouths or throats;
they are only valued by shape, by counts.
For cells do not have opinions or votes;
they are only valued by speed and amounts.

Too small to view, are cells really there?
Look *inside* . . . there's still a ways to go—
too small to view, cells are everywhere.
O World . . . this is just the start of the show!

To learn more about these sideshows and to see the original sideshows which inspired the poems and illustrations, visit:

Johnny Eck

The Johnny Eck Museum: www.johnnyeckmuseum.com

The Amazing Johnny Eck, traveling exhibit (MICA 2014)

Blaze Starr

Blaze Starr's Gems:
webarchive.org/web/20130518053733/http://blazestarrsgems.com

Blaze Starr: *My Life as Told to Huey Perry*
by Blaze Starr and Huey Perry (Preager Publishers, 1974)

Divine

The Official Website of Divine: www.divineofficial.com

Shock Value: A Tasteful Book about Bad Taste by John Waters
(Running Press, 2005)

Axl Rotten

Axl Rotten's Facebook Page: www.facebook.com/axlrottenecw

Axl Rotten's Twitter Account: twitter.com/axlrottenecw

Henrietta Lacks

The Immortal Life of Henrietta Lacks by Rebecca Skloot
(Broadway Books, 2011)

Henrietta Lacks Foundation: www.henriettalacksfoundation.org

Acknowledgments

Selections from the "Vessels" section of the book were previously published in *The Free State Review*.

The "Vessels" series received the Adele Holden New Voices Award, Morgan State University, Baltimore, Maryland (2014).

Special Thanks To

inspiring and supportive friends & family—

Sara Kelleher
Sam Janesko
John Hamer
The Anderson & Cottle Crews

the many other Baltimore-based 20th century creative minds we remember, including—

Adam Shelby White
Melissa Peverly
Harold Edward Smith Jr.

... and all of the artists and writers who keep creating, side-by-side, in spite of it all.

The Birth of "Baltimore Sideshow"

Childhood "besties," Katherine and Shannon began collaborative "side-shows" as far back as 1985 which resulted in volumes of what they playfully called "Comic Soaps." These whimsical diversions consisted of clippings from the local Sunday newspaper's "Funnies" section, augmented with personal doodles and superimposed with their own original captions and story lines. These endeavors served as a creative and emotional outlet for the aspiring writer and artist, taking teenage note writing to another level as the elaborate notes turned into stapled multi-paged "Comic Soap books."

The tradition they established at age fourteen has spanned over three decades since, albeit a lot less frequently than those first years, with the odd surprise Comic Soap annually or semi-annually gracing each others' mailboxes, once less than a mile away in their Baltimore suburban childhood homes, now 3,000 miles apart.

No friend, classmate, family member or topic was (or remains) off limits in their non-PC Comic Soap adventures, most especially each other, as they showed no qualms about making caricatures of and silly names for one another in their comical fantasies.

In 1988, just a few years after the beginnings of their Comic Soap "industry," Shannon and Katherine teamed up in an attempt at an illustrated book of poetry, but other sideshows of busy lives got in the way and resulted in only this one finished piece, "Detroit River, 1928."

More than thirty years later their dream to produce a book of their own original poems and artwork has finally found fruition in *Baltimore Sideshow*.

Detroit River, 1928

My grandfather's parents stand,
refusing to smile for the camera,
straight and stern,
their Missouri bodies
like soldiers at attention.
James Palmer has his hat
in his hand, looking forward.
Sara looks away,
perhaps at the city their
ship is approaching.
The calm beneath them at 50 ft
is now the same stagnant grey
as her homemade dress.

Their bodies are too big
for this city.
From here they look twice
the size of the buildings.
Too large for artists
to measure by.
Too stubborn
to shrink.

Katherine Cottle's Sideshows

Silica Mud Mask, Blue Lagoon, Iceland, 2017

Sideshows of the author, Katherine Cottle, include
spending time with her family and pets, researching
neglected history, observing, interdisciplinary
mapping, traveling, genealogy, discovering,
burning dinners, and creating Comic Soaps with Shannon.

Katherine is also the author of:

The Hidden Heart of Charm City: Baltimore Letters and Lives
(Nonfiction, 2019),
*I Remain Yours: Secret Mission Love Letters of My
Mormon Great-Grandparents, 1900-1903*
(Creative Nonfiction, 2014),
Halfway: A Journal through Pregnancy (Memoir, 2010),
and *My Father's Speech* (Poetry, 2008),

all published by Apprentice House/Loyola University Maryland and
available through Amazon.com or ApprenticeHouse.com.

More about her recent writing projects can be viewed at:
www.katherinecottle.com

Shannon Rowan's Sideshows

Sacred Circularities Hoop Dance retreat performance, Ubud, Bali, 2014

Sideshows of the illustrator, Shannon Rowan, include
fire dancing, hula hoop performing, sea kayaking,
trapeeze swinging, globetrotting, geopolitical & health
researching, guitar playing, singing, songwriting, rebelling,
protesting, cat wrangling, goat herding, daydreaming
and creating Comic Soaps with Katherine.

Shannon is also the author and illustrator of a children's book
titled *The Goldfish of Brandywine Farms*, found on Amazon.

More of her artwork can be viewed at:
www.shannonrowan.com

For hula hoop dance performance videos go to:
www.shapeshifterhoops.com